Praise for Kristopher Reisz's previous novels:

<u>*Unleashed*</u>

"This novel is sure to be a word-of-mouth favorite among older teens."

—*School Library Journal*

"Hot, wrenching, and wise, this book is fantastic!"

—Holly Black, author of *Tithe*

<u>*Tripping to Somewhere*</u>

"Readers willing to make the trip with all its strange turns will uncover a surprisingly sweet message about the power of love."

—*Publishers Weekly*

"The fast pace, earnest characters, and philosophical meanders kept me hooked from beginning to end."

—*GLBTFantasy.com*

The
Drowned
Forest

This book is dedicated to Johnny Cash
and Sister Rosetta Tharpe.

The Drowned Forest

Kristopher Reisz

Woodbury, Minnesota

First Edition
First Printing, 2014

Book design by Bob Gaul
Cover design by Lisa Novak
Cover image © iStockphoto.com/3763314/Arman Zhenikeyev

Flux, an imprint of Llewellyn Worldwide Ltd.

Library of Congress Cataloging-in-Publication Data
Reisz, Kristopher.
    The drowned forest/Kristopher Reisz.—First edition.
        pages cm
    Summary: "After her best friend Holly jumps off a river bluff and vanishes, fifteen-year-old Jane becomes convinced that the desperate, devouring mud creature who arises from the river is Holly, trapped and unaware she is dead"— Provided by publisher.
    ISBN 978-0-7387-3910-6
    [1. Supernatural—Fiction. 2. Dead—Fiction. 3. Christian life—Fiction. 4. Faith—Fiction. 5. Grief—Fiction. 6. Family life—Alabama—Fiction. 7. Alabama—Fiction.] I. Title.
    PZ7.R27848Dro 2014
    [Fic]—dc23
                                                        2013032699

Flux
Llewellyn Worldwide Ltd.
2143 Wooddale Drive
Woodbury, MN 55125-2989
www.fluxnow.com

Printed in the United States of America

Acknowledgments

I owe a huge debt of gratitude to my parents, James and Denise Reisz, as well as my friends Josh Olive and Leslie Crowe, for their support, encouragement, and endless patience in reading early drafts. (Also, Leslie, sorry about killing off the dog.) In addition, Haley Hardwick gave me more anecdotes about the lives of struggling musicians than I could ever fit in one book. My agent, Joe Monti, told me the ugly truths about the publishing world while still keeping me laughing. And finally, Brian Farrey-Latz, Sandy Sullivan, and everybody at Flux Books took in this redheaded stepchild of a story and treated it like their own.

This book couldn't have happened without y'all. Thank you.

One

But it's a beautiful day, Holly. It's the most beautiful day.

Pastor Wesley stands in the river, frog-green water swirling around his thighs. Sunlight ripples in his outstretched hands and across the white robes of those about to be baptized.

"…Nobody can carry these burdens on their own. We've all tried. All of us have struggled."

One of the converts sobs, head hanging against his chest. Others lift their arms to Heaven.

"We've come to set our burdens down. At long last. Knowing God will always shoulder them for us."

Tyler plucks out the opening hook on his guitar, and we raise our voices. *"I'm gonna lay down my heavy load, down by the riverside, down by the riverside, down by the riverside. I'm gonna lay down my heavy load…"*

This song is in our bones, the song we sing every River-call. People clap or lift their hands. Bodies sway with the grass.

Good church shoes churn up the thick red Alabama clay. Faye, a bouncing ball of taffeta, jumps around to a rhythm all her own. You see her, Holly?

"*I'm gonna put on my long white robe, down by the riverside, down by the riverside, down by the riverside...*"

Pastor Wesley takes the hand of the first convert, leading him into the water. He's lowered into the coldness, down into the dark and quiet of death.

Just for a second, though. Then he rises up again. He is reborn. The Spirit caresses him in tongues of holy flame. His struggles are over, and he knows it. I can see from his face that he knows it.

One by one, men and women, boys and girls, let who they used to be drown. One by one, the redeemed emerge from the river. Sometimes, spilling over with new life, they jerk and buck. The deacons hold them up, under their armpits, until they can walk to shore. They are washed clean in the blood of the Lamb. And this is the most beautiful day, Holly.

But my heart is shut to it all. I can't stop thinking about how, one month ago, you fell into the river and vanished. No singers lending you courage, no hugging afterward. Just the cold and dark and endless quiet.

Your pa-paw stands on the edge of the crowd wearing clean jeans and a bolo tie. He sees me looking and smiles. I smile back, then Faye slips in the dewy grass. I scoop her up before she starts crying. Whispering in her ear, I coax her to sing.

"*Well, I'm gonna meet all of my brethren, down by the riverside, down by the riverside, down by the riverside...*"

I sing as loud as I can, but I can't feel tongues of holy flame. I'm just dizzy and wilting in the heat and deviled by sweat bees.

Tyler stretches the song out while one last buzz-cut boy and his mom get baptized. While they're led off to change into dry clothes, the congregation drifts toward the picnic shelter. Fried chicken, steaming hot rolls, sweet white corn, and plenty more crowd the wooden tables. Everybody starts filling their plates; everybody except your pa-paw. He pushes against the crowd, going to clap Tyler on the back.

I need to say hey, but not right now. Instead I turn to Faye, asking, "Ready for some chicken?"

Faye gets to carry the drinks. I load our plates with food and we sit with Mom, Dad, and Yuri. The wind is sweet—smelling of grass. Our picnic blanket flutters, held down with rocks. The fried chicken skin crackles like tracing paper between my teeth. I tear through it, and a sputter of hot juice hits my tongue.

Know why Baptists make such good fried chicken, Holly? Because we have to. We can't drink, gamble, or cuss. That's a lot of carnal urges that have to be satisfied through chicken. If you took this away, we'd go crazy.

"Jane, you say hi to Tyler?" Dad asks, cutting Yuri's chicken into pieces with his pocketknife.

"I will."

"Well, tell him how great he played."

"Yes, sir." I tuck a napkin into the collar of Faye's dress. She's got her corncob clutched in both pink fists, and the niblets are flying. "He doesn't have to show off, though. All those noodley-noodley parts in the middle."

Dad laughs. "That's just his style. Every musician needs their own style."

Remember when you played at last year's Rivercall, Holly? You played the song clean. You knew that "Down by the Riverside" doesn't need noodley-noodley parts to be beautiful. It's more beautiful without them.

"I'm just thankful he came," Mom says. "Go say hello."

"I will. Let me eat first."

"Take your plate with you. Jane…" Her voice drops to a whisper. "Remember what Dr. Haq said? You're not supposed to isolate."

"I'm not—yes, ma'am." I have to show that I'm keeping it together, so I don't argue and stand up to go over. Mom adds, "And tell Tim he better get some food before it's gone. I'm not fixing lunch today."

My brother is exploring the shore with his friends. I shout at him to go eat, but they're busy flipping over rocks and watching whatever scurries or slithers out from underneath. I'm not going to chase after them if they're having fun.

Tyler's talking to Bo now. Where's your pa-paw, Holly? I search the picnickers, but I guess he left already. Tomorrow, I'll stop by your house, just check in on him. I know, I know. I've been saying that since your funeral, but this time I really will. Tomorrow. No excuses.

Except your house must still smell like you. I don't think I can walk in there without falling apart. But I'll try. Tomorrow. I promise, promise, promise.

4

"Hey, Jane!" Bo waves me over. "I was telling Tyler how awesome he was today."

"Yeah, you were great." I go to hug Tyler, but he hesitates. Then he reaches out, but I hesitate, one arm hanging in the air. It's like we're trying to reach around the empty space where you should be.

Tyler says, "I saw your mom and dad. I was gonna go say hi."

"You should. They ask about you a lot."

"Sorry I haven't been around lately. I just—"

"No, I mean, they've just been worried about you."

We fall into stiff silence, smiles frozen in place. I say, "You really did play great."

"Thanks."

More silence.

Tyler says, "I did email you a while—"

"Yeah, I got it. I just—"

"Don't worry about it."

"Sorry."

"Don't worry about it. Seriously."

I smooth out imaginary wrinkles in my dress. Why is talking to him so hard? How can I have nothing to say after all the youth group stuff we've done together? After all the times he's been at my house, wrestling with Tim on the living room carpet? He was your boyfriend, Holly; he loved you as much as I did.

But everything's strange now, and everybody's a stranger. Even Tyler.

"Okay. Well, I'm going to get some food before it's all

gone," Bo says. He squeezes both our shoulders, telling Tyler, "You have a real gift. Thanks for sharing it."

"No problem."

Bo's the one who asked Tyler to play today, wasn't he? It's exactly the sort of youth ministry thing he'd do. Half a dozen other musicians in the congregation, but Bo reaches out to the guy who hasn't been to church in weeks.

"And Tyler, I'd really like to talk about getting you into the praise band," Bo adds.

Tyler shakes his head. "No. Thanks, but I don't really think I could keep up with their schedule."

"Well, maybe we could just have you fill in every once in a while. Like I said, Tyler, you have an incredible—"

"I said no."

The snap in Tyler's voice startles Bo. He laughs to cover it up. "Okay. No problem. But still, thanks for coming out today. Jane, take care now."

He heads off, and Tyler says, "Guess I better get some chicken too," trying to slip away gracefully.

"You can have mine if you want." I offer him the thigh on my plate. No matter how awkward this feels, I do want him to stay.

"I can't steal your food."

"Whatever. Since when?"

Tyler laughs, and there's a glimmer of what things were like before. He takes the chicken and my roll. We sit on a driftwood tree worn smooth as bone. Pulling off my sandals, I press my toes into the water and sandy soil. The Tennessee River rushes across four states, but here, behind Wilson

Dam, it slows down and swells up. The river turns into fat, lazy Wilson Lake. That makes it a perfect spot for a picnic. It makes it the perfect spot to talk and share food and try to reconnect with Tyler.

We chat about the weather and how bad the mosquitoes are. When we run out of easy things to talk about, Tyler picks up his guitar. He plays some little riff and asks, "So, you doing okay? Really?"

"Yeah. I mean, it's not like I'm not sad, but ... I've been praying a lot."

Tyler nods without looking up from his guitar.

"How about you? Doing okay?" I ask.

"Not really, no." He starts into the same song again, the lonely riff leading into chords sick with reverb.

"I know you're sad right now, but ... I mean, I am too but ... when you're at the end of your rope, you just have to tie a knot of faith and hold on. I mean, we just ... we ... "

Tyler's song squeezes my chest, making it hard to breathe, impossible to speak. It holds me trapped, watching the guitar strings flicker like dragonfly wings under his fingers. There's no noodley-noodley parts, no big finish. Tyler just drops his palm across the strings, and the song vanishes.

"I need to get this stuff packed away." He waves a hand toward the church's battered amp and the cords snaking through the grass. "But it was good seeing you. Say hi to your mom and dad and everybody, okay?"

"You don't want to—"

"No, I'm gonna get this stuff packed away and head on out. But good seeing you."

"Yeah, you too."

"Thanks for the chicken."

"Sure." Another awkward hug, and he walks away.

I turn to watch a barge cutting down the middle of the lake, heading toward the dam. Once it enters the lock, dam operators will lower it to the other side, where the river runs narrow and quick again—a hundred tons of steel and cargo, along with a couple thousand gallons of water, dropping five stories in a few minutes. From the shore, though, the barge seems to drift along ghost-silent, wavering in the hot air. The dam's groans and shrieks of metal have a hollow quality, like they're not quite real.

After another minute, I pick up my sandals and walk back. With most people finished eating, Bo is getting some of the kids together for a water-balloon toss. I edge around them and return to our family's picnic blanket.

Mom asks, "So how's Tyler?"

"Good."

"I hope he starts coming to church again."

He won't. He was doing a favor for Bo today, that's all. "He's still pretty sad."

"Well, of course, but he's got to stop running away from God and let Him catch up."

Dad adds, "Email him tonight. Make sure he knows he'll always be welcomed back."

I roll my eyes. "He knows."

"Never hurt anybody to hear it." Dad rubs my back. "Tyler needs God, honey. That means he needs you."

"Yes, sir."

Holly, I'm sorry. I know how bad Tyler's hurting, but I can't be his shepherd. I can barely keep myself together.

Yuri pushes his plate away and starts rocking. Mom hasn't shaved him in a couple days, and bits of food stick to the stubble around his lips. Dabbing them off with my napkin, I ask, "You want some pie, buddy?"

"Pie."

"Mmm … ice cream on top?"

"Ice cream." He stops rocking. "An' pie."

I get back up to get dessert. Out on the river, something breaks the surface, catching my eye—an old Styrofoam cooler, slimy green-black with algae. I slow down, shield my eyes with my hand. A blossoming brown wake moves toward the bank—sediment and trash tumbling up from the bottom. Tim and his friends are too busy playing to notice the flip-flop pop up a few feet away.

A loud wet smack makes one of the boys yelp, and every head whips around. The boys scramble backward. Tyler runs toward the bank, and I'm on his heels.

"C'mon, guys. Keep away from it." Tyler steers the kids behind him. But Tim is crouched down, reaching toward the catfish. Before I can shout, Tyler catches his wrist. "Watch it. Don't want to catch one of those spines." He scoops Tim up and passes him over to me.

"Jane, see it?" Tim asks.

I nod, squeezing my brother against me. The catfish probably weighs more than Tim. It's the size of a Rottweiler. Fleshy whiskers taste the air. Too-human eyes—pupils and irises surrounded by white—have shrunk to pinpoints in the sudden sunlight.

Gruh ... Gruh ... The thing's croak sounds like old bones splintering. Its mouth is a lipless gash, dripping wads of mud. The thing already smells dead. It's carried the rotten smell of the lake bottom up with it. It still thrashes, though, driving itself higher up onto the rocks.

Gruh ...

"Whoa." Adults crowd around us. I feel a hand on my shoulder. "Jane, take your brother and ... man, that girl's gotta be a hundred pounds."

"Check out the hook scars; she's been around awhile."

"Wonder why she beached herself like that."

"Must be sick. Fish'll do that sometimes if they're sick and dying."

The fish slaps its tail against the mud. People jump back. There's more nervous laughter, then someone says, "Let's get these kids out of here. Come on, kids, let's get some pie."

They herd Tim and the other boys back to the picnic shelter. None of them notice the giant catfish cough something up. A ring.

Gruh ... Gruh ...

Tyler asks, "Jane? You okay?"

I step closer to the beast—raw pink gills pumping as it suffocates—and snatch the treasure from the mud.

"Jane, what—"

"It's Holly's ring." I rub away the grime. "Tyler, it's the ring you gave her. It's ... Tyler, it's ... "

Tyler takes it with shaking hands. He turns it over—the

simple silver band with a cut-out cross—lost to the depths, now returned.

Grace fills me. I laugh out loud, then want to cry. Thank you, Holly, thank you for this miracle. I couldn't have kept going much longer. I love you, I love you.

"What...? Jane, look." Letters are scratched thin and bright into the tarnished silver. Tyler cleans the ring with his shirttail. It reads, *HELP*.

Two

Memories flow together. Things sink to the sunless bottom. But the day I met you always bobs close to the surface, Holly. My mouth still goes dry when I think about it. I'd never met a kid whose parents were dead.

Mom let me wear my new ladybug dress; I was so excited about that. She waited until we were in the car before telling me your parents had passed away. You lived with your grandparents now, Mr. and Mrs. Alton from church.

"How'd they die?"

Mom shook her head. "It's not important. Listen. She might be sad and not feel like playing. She might even start crying. But you have to be nice no matter what. Can you do that? You need to be like the Good Samaritan."

"But were they sick?"

"I told you it doesn't matter. Don't ask. Don't even mention it to her."

So I didn't know about the car wreck yet, the shriek of

metal and glass that killed two grown-ups and left a seven-year-old without a scratch. I didn't know you were a miracle in the flesh. All I knew was my stomach suddenly hurt and I wanted to go home.

We pulled up to that prim brick house skirted with impatiens. Your me-maw came out to the porch as we walked up. "Oh, look at all the ladybugs! So summery!"

I tried to stick close to Mom, but she nudged me out into the backyard. And there you were—crouching under the hydrangeas, mostly knees and elbows and bits of leaf stuck in your hair.

You would always be mostly knees and elbows, Holly.

When I walked over, you turned away. Picking cream-colored blossoms off the bushes, you pretended not to notice me. "Hi. I'm Jane." I held my scrubbed pink hand out for your grubby one. You wouldn't look up.

"Want to have a wedding? You can be the bride if you want."

You shook your head. Busy, busy, busy, sorting the flower petals into piles.

I walked back to the sliding glass door. Mom and your me-maw chatted in the kitchen. Looking over your me-maw's shoulder, Mom hit me with a hard glare. I knew better than to try going back inside.

Instead, I sat on the concrete steps, tearing blades of grass to bits. I kept having to move away from the bees murmuring through the clover. I was getting hot and mad, and this place was boring, and I couldn't be like the Good Samaritan because you wouldn't even talk to me.

You pulled off one of the hydrangea's powder-puff flower clusters, studying it carefully. Squinting against the sun, you studied me. Finally you walked over, holding the cluster in your hand. You spoke in a hoarse whisper. "This can be my bouquet."

"Okay. But you have to throw it and let me catch it."

"Okay. Then you can get married."

We played wedding all morning. I didn't ask about your parents, and you didn't mention them. I wasn't afraid anymore, though.

Days, months, and years flow together after that. Growing up, we lived like swallows of the air who neither sow nor reap. We roamed a backyard full of castles and zoos, then helped your pa-paw dig up the hydrangeas to make space for the sunporch. That old dry-erase board became our classroom, and you always got to be the teacher because you went to real school. No matter how much it pleased God to see me home-schooled, I wanted to eat in a cafeteria so bad.

And have a food fight. Just one good food fight, and my life would be complete.

Dad took us out in the boat and taught us to water-ski on Wilson Lake. We caught fish and cleaned them ourselves. Sometimes summer storms caught us out on the water. Saw-toothed waves the color of iron gnashed at the boat. The wind howled. But we tipped our faces to the stinging rain and howled right back, thrilled by all of lashing creation.

We heard stories about the giant catfish living in the deep black water at the lake bottom, squeezed down between the roots of submerged trees and under the foundations of flooded sharecropper cabins. Ancient scavenger-demons full of bile and spines, they were half-mythical beasts. But every once in a while, a fisherman wrestled one of the massive channel cats up into the sunlight. It would get in the newspaper then, with photos for everybody to gape at.

We dove off Swallow's Nest Bluff a thousand times.

The bluff is one of those secret children's places. Grown-ups can't find it. The first time anyone goes, they need a cousin or older neighborhood kid to lead them past the *No Trespassing* signs and down into the wild land the city owns but has forgotten about. The path is just a line of dirt stomped out between blackberry bushes. Near the bluff, the thorny vines curl into circles and weave themselves together to mimic Jesus's crown. Berries dangle from the crowns, as dark and glossy as blood drops. They're the most delicious fruit I've ever tasted. I've eaten them until juice stained my chin and ran down my arms, and I still wanted more.

Push past the bushes, and there's Swallow's Nest Bluff, a wedge of red limestone shoving out into Wilson Lake like the prow of a ship. And there's the squat pine tree sending wrist-thick roots over the edge of the bluff. And there's the tire swing, its rubber cracked from the sun.

When we were little, it took all our courage just to swing out over the lake, watching the land drop away, watching the swallows that built their nests on the bluff's tilting face dart and wheel below us. But soon enough, we trusted ourselves enough to jump. We waited until the tire reached the vertex of its arc over the water, then kicked away, tumbling, flipping, jackknifing, cannonballing, and swan-diving into the water again and again.

When I told my cousin I'd finally jumped off Swallow's Nest Bluff, I was swelling with pride. But she didn't know what I was talking about. She'd already grown up too much and couldn't remember the bluff. It became our place then, Holly. It became our wilderness to scurry through—to test ourselves against—dirty, wet, and laughing our heads off. I remember the sunlight filtering through the pines, touching the fine hair on your arms, legs, and the back of your neck. The light made them burn like filaments.

We had bad times. We had arguments and weeks when we were too busy for each other. And your raw-nerve days, scratching lyrics into the dry skin of your arm with a pen cap or whatever. But when I try to think about them, all I can remember is you doing a hair-whipping backflip into the water, a miracle in the flesh.

We dove off the bluff a thousand times and never got hurt. Nobody dies the thousand-and-first time they do something. It's stupid, Holly. It's not fair.

It's just not fair.

Three

Dad drives through downtown and swings into the church parking lot, jostling me out of happier days and back into this one. There's a mountain of stuff to unload. A steady trickle of people carry coolers, steam trays, buckets, and bins back to the cinder-block storage shed. Everything is stenciled with *Magnolia Street Baptist Church—Florence, Alabama.*

Tyler's truck, dusty and rumbling, swings into the space beside me. Stepping out, he whispers, "So what now?"

"Just help unload everything, then we can find Pastor Wesley."

We tried getting Pastor Wesley alone at the park, but couldn't. And I'm sorry, Holly, but I can't start talking about fish delivering rings and messages from the dead in the middle of Rivercall. Most people would think I'm crazy. The ones who believe me would freak out. Heck, it's freaking me out.

But Pastor Wesley is a man of God. He's smart, calm, and

he knows how to read the signs and exhortations of the Lord. He'll know what's happening.

Dad calls out, "Come on, guys. Let's get this done. Tyler, help us old men out." Dad has two stainless steel urns in the back of the van. He tips one out, and Tyler hurries to catch it. Mr. Olsen grabs the other one. I take the Rubbermaid bin full of tablecloths. Dad tries to give Yuri the few that fell out, but Yuri won't take them.

"That's okay, pal. Go with Jane."

We carry the stuff to the community hall storeroom, then head outside again. Everyone's full of chicken and starting to droop, so nobody's going to work too hard except the kids playing tag. People lounge around, visiting. Boys tease girls.

Tyler says, "I don't see Pastor Wesley."

"Probably in his office. Come on." But then manic Hannah Marie rushes up, squeezing Tyler around the middle. "Hey! You played so great today!"

Ashley, Jonathan, and Brooke come up behind her. "You're getting sunburned," Ashley tells me.

"Yeah." I touch the stinging skin around my eyes. I don't care about this, I don't care, don't care. But I have to smile and make-believe everything's okay. "You are too, a little."

"Am I?" Ashley looks up, trying to see her own forehead. That makes Jonathan laugh, and Ashley smacks him.

"So how have you been?" Jonathan asks.

"Good." I nod. "Pretty good."

"Good, good. That's real good." He nods back. "But listen, uh, we were wondering about the winter mission trip. Weren't you sort of in charge of that before ... you know."

"Yeah. I still am." Go! Please, God, just make them go! "It's the first weekend in December. I haven't sent out an email, but I will."

"Cool. Are we building another house?"

"We're going to try for two this time."

"Two? Seriously?"

"Yeah, but we're going to get some help from another youth group down from … Ardmore, I think. I'll have more details when I send the email. I'll get to it soon, promise." I force a smile, looking for a chance to edge away. But now Hannah Marie is boxing with Tyler, throwing punches into his open palms and trying to get him to say he'll go on the trip with us.

"Remember we put on that skit last year and you were the CSI guy? That was so much fun!"

"Yeah, I … I just … I don't know."

"Tyler, please come." Hannah Marie stops boxing, weaves her skinny fingers into his thick ones. "I know, with Holly and all, you feel like you're alone right now."

"That's not—" He tries to pull his hands free, but she clings to him.

"You have to stop running from God and let Him catch up, you know?"

"Let go!" Tyler jerks free. Hannah Marie opens her mouth, but nothing comes out. A loud crash makes everybody jump.

Yuri has knocked over one of the terra-cotta planters. He studies the smashed pieces spilling dirt and hibiscus leaves across the walk.

"Yuri! That wasn't—"

Yuri walks away, flapping one hand and raising a shrill whine. I catch his wrist. The whine goes higher, and he tries prying my fingers loose. He's got a stomachache or he's tired or maybe Tyler's shout upset him, and he doesn't want to be touched now.

"That wasn't nice, Yuri." I hold him as loosely as I can. "Did you eat too much?"

He quiets himself, still plucking at my fingers. "Leggo."

Behind us, our friends have moved in. Tyler and Jonathan gather up the pottery shards. Brooke shoos a couple little kids back, but Yuri's whine has brought Dad and some other grown-ups trotting around the corner.

"Oh no. Guys, I'm sorry. It didn't hit anybody, did it? Tyler, let me do that." Dad starts into the usual apologies, worn thin from daily use.

But we're at church, so what's to apologize for? These people have loved Yuri since our parents brought him home from Russia. He's their brother in Christ, just like he's mine by adoption.

I take Yuri to the steps to sit down, and he lets me hold his hand. I squeeze it, and he squeezes mine back. I squeeze his twice, and he squeezes mine twice. I squeeze his three times, and he squeezes mine three times. We play our favorite game, all the way up to eight squeezes, then Yuri loses count. I laugh. "Ha! I win, buddy!"

Yuri gives one of his bright toddler-laughs, eyes clamped shut with pleasure. He grows quiet again, and I lean close to smooth down his hair. I whisper, "Something's happening.

Something with Holly. And I don't know what it is, and I'm scared."

Yuri turns, and we watch the others clean up the dirt and broken planter. We're at church. Church is not a doctrine; it's not a pretty building. Church is anywhere a nineteen-year-old who can't tie his shoes brings out the best in people.

We're at church, and I shouldn't feel as lonely as I do. I shouldn't be lost inside my own head all the time talking to you. I need to let these people help me, Holly. Pastor Wesley is a Godly man. He'll see the truth in this. He'll see the signs and know what to do.

Maybe God is trying to show me that, acting through the one sinless soul here.

I stand up to kiss Yuri's temple, telling him, "I love you." His serene expression doesn't change. He studies me with those sweet brown eyes, irises so dark they blend with the pupil. He has the prettiest lashes I've ever seen on a boy.

As soon as Dad gets the dirt swept off the walk, I walk up to him, leading Yuri. "He's probably just tired. If you want to take him home, I can finish helping out here, and Tyler'll give me a ride home later. I bet Faye's worn out too."

"Well ... " Dad looks at Yuri, then Tyler. "You don't mind?"

"Huh? No. No, be happy to," Tyler stammers, caught off-guard by my surprise move.

"Well ... yeah. Probably for the best."

We round up Tim and Faye. Lifting Faye into her car seat, Mom slips me a crisp twenty. "Why don't you and Tyler get some coffee or something afterward?"

"Sure. Thanks." They're glad I'm catching up with Tyler, glad I'm doing anything besides sleeping all day and eating dinner in my room. I keep my happy face on and wave goodbye as Dad pulls out of the parking lot.

Once they're gone, we head back to the community hall, this time heading straight upstairs, passing empty offices and the Sunday school classroom. The puppet theater is still in the corner. Remember putting on goofy shows for just each other? I bet it's the same puppets piled behind there: Mother Goose, one little pig, and the threadbare wolf.

Pastor Wesley's door is open, but he's on the phone. He smiles when he sees us, waves us in, then turns back to his conversation. "Absolutely, but our secretary can give you a better answer on that... uh-huh... uh-huh..."

I flex my fingers, twist my feet into the lush blue carpet, getting anxious.

Hanging up, Pastor Wesley scribbles a note on his desk calendar. "Tyler, you were incredible today," he says without looking up.

"Thanks... thank you, sir."

"I meant to tell you at the park, but I got tied up. But really, you amazed me."

I don't know anybody besides Pastor Wesley who pronounces the period at the end of each sentence. At least I hear it in my head, like the bang of a gavel, opinion becoming fact and the end of all argument.

"Sit, guys, sit. Jane, how are you?"

"Good. Um, we actually need to talk to you about Rivercall. About that catfish."

He lets out a two-tone whistle. "What do you think it was? Ninety pounds? A hundred?"

"Well, it was pretty big. Plus, also, it had Holly's ring in its mouth."

Pastor Wesley stares at us. "Holly...Alton?"

I nod. "It dropped it onto the rocks. Like it was delivering it. And it..."

Tyler is rubbing his thumb across the ring. I nudge him, and he sets it on Pastor Wesley's desk. "It says *HELP*," Tyler finishes for me. "See?"

Pastor Wesley picks up the ring, sets it down again. His eyes are blank; his mouth is a straight, thin line. He asks me, "You were good friends with Holly, weren't you?"

"Uh...yes, sir. She was my best friend."

"I know you've had some trouble since she passed, making sense of the tragedy."

"Yes, but...right now, I'm worried about Holly. She's trying to tell us something, but we don't know what this ring means."

Pastor Wesley continues on his own train of thought. "Your parents actually came to see me last week. They've been worried about you, Jane. I've meant to schedule some time with you and your family. But with Rivercall and everything..." He waves a hand over his desk calendar.

No, no, no, Pastor Wesley has to see the signs. My fingers strangle one another in my lap. "I'm not crazy, sir. Holly needs help, but we don't know what to do. We don't know...please, you have to help."

"Jane, I want to help you. But I don't believe this is a message from Holly's ghost."

"Who else would it be from? This is Holly's ring!"

"I don't know. But sometimes, in times of grief especially, people see what they *want* to see the most. It's called magical thinking."

"I'm not making this up!" My face starts to burn with embarrassment. "Tyler saw the catfish drop it too." I look to Tyler for support.

He nods slightly. "I did. Really."

"Jane, nobody's accusing anybody of anything. But there—"

"Pastor Wesley, please, please, we have to help Holly."

"But there could be lots of explanations for this ring. I don't want you getting worked up over nothing."

"It's not nothing! Holly needs help! I know! I can feel it!"

"Jane, calm down. You need to listen to me right now."

His voice is placid, so gentle it infuriates me. Jumping up, I turn and walk out.

"Jane, please," Pastor Wesley calls at my back. "Tyler! Please come back."

I take the stairs two at a time. Tyler keeps close at me heels. "Where are you going?" he hisses. "You're the one who wanted to talk to—"

At the foot of the staircase, Brooke looks up. "Um … is Pastor Wesley calling—"

"Okay, see you later." I wave at her but never slow down. Shoving the door open, I stomp out into the parking lot.

"Jane, you're the one who wanted to talk to Wesley," Tyler says. "Now what? Now what do we do?"

"I don't know. But we're not going to do nothing."

"Then what?"

"I don't know!"

People glance over. Tyler leads me to his truck and unlocks the passenger-side door for me. I say, "He's a man of God. He's supposed to know the true signs of prophecy."

"I know," Tyler says.

"Come on, let's get out of here."

"And go where?"

"I don't know. Just go, okay? Just … I can't be here right now."

Tyler starts the truck and pulls out of the parking lot. Moving makes me feel a little better. As we cruise down College Street, I mock Pastor Wesley's lofty tone. "'There could be lots of explanations for this ring.'" I smash my elbow into the door panel so hard, numb pain shoots into my chest. A thought hits me. "The ring! Did we leave it in Pastor Wesley's office?"

Tyler shakes his head and digs it out of his jeans pocket, keeping his eyes on the road. I take it from him and turn it between my fingers. Looking at it, feeling so useless, physically hurts. "It's Holly's ring. Two people saw a fish spit it out. It has *HELP* written on it. Name one! Name one other explanation for that!"

"I'm not arguing with you."

"Tyler, what are we going to do? What is Holly trying to tell us?"

"I don't know. Should we go talk to your folks?"

I shake my head. "I don't think they'd believe us either."

"Why not? And why did they talk to Pastor Wesley last week?"

"It's just … it's nothing."

Tyler sighs, frustrated with me. "It can't be just nothing. Just tell me."

My face burns hot, but I need to confess. "I just … I haven't been doing that great. And they're sorta worried about me."

"Like what? What's going on?"

"I've just been praying a lot."

"Your parents are worried because you're praying a lot. *Your* parents?"

Staring at my hands, I say, "Sometimes for hours, like two or three hours straight." I don't mention the even-longer crying jags in between, but still, I want Tyler to understand. "And, well, Tuesday, Tim kept bothering me. And I threatened to shove him down the stairs, but he just wouldn't leave me alone. So I dragged him over to the top of the staircase and lifted him off his feet. I wasn't going to really do it, but I was mad. And then I locked myself in my room and wouldn't talk to anybody, and Dad had to take the doorknob off."

Tyler glances at me, then back at the road. Several seconds of silence pass. Then he starts snickering.

"Stop!" I smack his beefy arm. "It's not funny."

"It is, a little."

"No, it's not. Stop laughing. You're making me laugh." My

shoulders bob up and down. "He can't get the doorknob back on, either. I've been using pliers to open my door all week."

That makes Tyler let out an open-mouthed bray, and you know how infectious his laugh is, Holly. Finally, I gather myself enough to say, "But after that, they called Pastor Wesley and they called this psychiatrist, Dr. Haq. We had to all go to this family therapy session and there's another one scheduled for next week and … it's no big deal, but they're already worried about me. If I tell them about this, they'll think I've flipped."

Tyler nods and drums his palms against the steering wheel, thinking. The tune he was playing at Rivercall while we sat together is stuck in my head, its sad little melody running over and over.

"Mr. Alton!" Tyler says. "We'll go talk to Holly's pa-paw. If she's trying to talk to us, maybe she's tried talking to him already."

"That's actually a good idea."

"'Actually'?"

"You can turn around in this gas station. Come on."

Tyler steers into a gas station and turns around. We fall into stiff silence again, nothing but wheels on the road and the shimmering heat above the highway as it rolls out of town.

Then Tyler says, "Hey. Sorry you're having such a rough time."

"Thanks."

"If you ever want to talk to somebody about it … you know, like … "

"I know. Thanks." If I need to talk to somebody, I can

talk to Tyler. He'll be awkward and embarrassed and useless, but he'll still listen. That's something. Actually, it's a lot.

Foster Mill Road curls away from downtown like a morning glory tendril. We drive into the hot hungry green, kudzu swallowing fences and cloaking the trees. When your house swings into view, I remember playing in the backyard. And watching *Grease* every sleepover. Then in the morning, we'd cook waffles and watch it again, or maybe *Les Miz*.

Tyler groans. "Nobody home."

I look at him, then back at the house. Your pa-paw's truck is gone. A pile of newspapers in blue plastic bags lies at the head of the driveway, and the hungry green has spread here too, with ragged grass growing to the second porch step.

"What happened? Where is he?"

Tyler shakes his head. We climb out and walk up to the porch. While Tyler knocks on the door, I walk around peeking through windows. Nothing moves inside. Your bedroom looks just the way it did the day you died, Holly. The bed sheets are rumpled, and that heart collage you made in art class hangs on the closet door. A cardinal feather marks your place in the book you were reading so you could get back to it later.

Peeking into your room hurts, Holly. I want to go home. I want to hide under my covers and sleep. But we've got to find your pa-paw first. Walking back around to the porch, I flutter the neck of my dress to let some cool air in. This heat is like being wrapped in damp gauze.

Tyler sits on the glider, pushing with the toe of his loafer. Back, forth, back, forth.

"He talked to you at Rivercall. Did he mention . . . ?"

Tyler shakes his head.

"Well, think for a second!"

"Jane, he didn't say anything."

Turning with a huff, I walk to the end of the driveway and count the newspapers. There's four of them, dewwrinkled in their plastic bags. I walk over to the neighbors, but they aren't any help. Mrs. Lewis says he comes back every few days but never stays the night. The Devines across the street didn't even notice he was gone, just that the grass was getting awfully tall.

I walk back. Still sitting in the glider, Tyler asks, "Well?"

I shake my head.

"He was at Rivercall, so we know he didn't move to Alaska at least," Tyler says. "I guess we'll have to wait until next Sunday. Talk to him at church."

"What if Holly can't wait a week?"

"Then tell me what to do."

I drop my head in my hands. "I kept meaning to visit him. If I'd gone once, we might know where he is. I kept saying I would and saying I would, but…"

"Yeah, me too," Tyler says.

"It's just hard. Coming here and knowing she's not here anymore." I take your ring out and play with it, rolling it between my fingers.

"I know, I know."

"So what are we going to do?"

Tyler shrugs and stares into the weeds swallowing the flower beds.

On the road again, we drive back past Veterans Park. I

stare out at the swelling belly of land and the red-shimmering river beyond it.

"Think Pastor Wesley'll call our parents?" I ask. "Tell them all the stuff we told him?"

"I don't know. Probably."

"They're going to freak out."

"So? Let them."

"Tyler, they already think I'm losing it."

"But you're not." Tyler takes the tarnished ring from me, holds it between two thick fingertips. "I saw a catfish drop this ring. Is that what you saw?"

I nod. "But—"

"I can see it has *HELP* written on it. Is that what you see?"

I nod, stuffing my trembling hands under my thighs.

"You sure? You sure it's not magical thinking?"

"Yeah. I'm sure."

"Then it doesn't matter what Pastor Wesley thinks, right? It doesn't matter what your parents or anybody thinks. We saw what we saw. We're not losing it. Holly's soul is trapped in the river somehow. And she needs us, and we can't worry about what anybody else thinks, okay?"

"Yeah."

"For Holly."

"For Holly, yeah."

He tucks the ring into his pocket again, then gives me a bolstering punch in the arm. We turn onto the road that crosses the top of Wilson Dam, heading toward the southern shore of the lake and my house. The water has turned molten in the sunlight. Staring down at it, I hear Tyler's melody in my head again, an ugly earworm burrowing into my brain. "That tune you played? It's been stuck in my head all day."

"Oh, 'The Drowned Forest'?" Tyler laughs. "Sorry."

"Just fits with how today's gone, I guess."

"I've been working on it with Ultimate Steve. He's got this great drum break, this sorta *dum dum da-da-dum* thing for it."

When did Tyler start hanging out with Steve the Nine-Digit Idiot again? I bite my tongue. "So why is it called 'The Drowned Forest'?"

"Well, it's named for, y'know, the lake."

"Oh."

"It's kind of sick, I know."

"Yeah, a little."

When the government dammed up the river many decades ago, all that backed-up water needed somewhere to go. It flooded acres of pine forest, farms, churches, graveyards, whole communities, creating Wilson Lake. The lake is a great place to fish and ski and swim. But if you swim down and down, past where the water turns suddenly cold, down and down into the slow, strange heartbeat of the river, you find yourself in the pines—dead trees preserved by the cold and dark. Black branches bloom algae and colonies of mussels. The forest has become the dominion of monster catfish and all the slithering things swarming without number.

The trees make it impossible to dredge the lake. When you drowned, they didn't even try to bring up your body. It makes me sick to my stomach thinking about you down there all alone, Holly. Lost in the drowned forest.

Four

Go thou to the sea, and cast an hook, and take up the fish that first cometh up; and when thou hast opened his mouth, thou shalt find a piece of money: that take, and give unto them for me and thee.

"Jane! Come slice these tomatoes for me."

"Yes, ma'am." The only footnote says that the "piece of money" would have been a silver shekel, worth four drachmas. How the heck does that help us?

"Jane, I need help here," Mom calls again.

"Okay. Give me one second." My finger moves back up to the beginning of the verse.

"Jane, your mom asked you to do something." Dad sits on the floor, trying to keep Yuri interested in their word games. "Your studying can wait."

The Bible drops to the coffee table. I stalk into the kitchen without looking at him.

Spaghetti bubbles on the stove. Steam swirls below the

oven hood. The tomatoes are from Dad's garden, and pieces of fuzzy green stem still poke up from their navels. When Jesus and Peter needed to pay their temple tax, Peter caught a fish with money in its mouth. Is that some clue to what's happening now? I cut the tomatoes into wedges, pulp oozing between my fingers.

"When you're done, Tim needs you to look over his math work."

I groan. "I'm kind of doing something right now."

"What, Jane? What's more important than helping your brother?"

"It's ... just ... nothing." I glance over at Tim doing his worksheet at the kitchen table. "I'll help you in a sec, okay, buddy?"

Tim gives me two thumbs-up. Mom says, "And slow down, honey. You'll cut yourself."

"I know what I'm doing." I pare a bruise out of the tomato's drum-tight flesh.

At least Pastor Wesley didn't call my parents. But still, he should be guiding us through this. It's on him that he couldn't hear the truth.

"Jane, give me the knife if you're not going to be careful."

"I'm being careful! You yell at me to come do this, then you hover over me like I'm six. Let me do it."

Mom reaches for the knife. "Jane, give me—"

I jerk back. The blade skates across the edge of her palm, and Mom's yelp silences the chatter in my head. Clutching her hand—blood runs and smears—Mom glares at me like she hates me. Everybody rushes up, talking at once.

"What happened?" Tim asks.

"Mom? What happened?"

"Nothing. Just an accident."

"Let me see. What happened?" Dad tries to take charge.

"I'm fine. Take the sauce off the stove, or it'll burn."

"Mom." I speak above the rest. "Mom, I'm sorry."

Her lips press together until they're white. "If you weren't acting like a brat, it wouldn't have happened."

Mom? Something happened at Rivercall.

"Not one of the good towels."

Dad shakes his head. "I don't care about towels."

"I do. Get one of the old ones from the linen closet."

Something happened, Dad. I need help. The words bunch in my throat, aching to be said. But I can't say them. Mom and Dad will think I'm insane.

"There's antibiotic ointment in the cabinet," Mom tells Tim. "And the big bandages. No, behind there."

I walk away. Nobody notices except Yuri, but he doesn't say anything. Grabbing my Bible, I go upstairs.

The moment I'm in my bedroom and it's finally quiet, I remember the mission trip email.

Dang it, who cares about the stupid email right now?

But if I don't take care of it, nobody else will. I've spent my whole life helping to take care of my brothers and sister, and it's given me a deep love of order, lists, and Post-its. So I'm the youth group leader. I'm in charge of the winter mission trip and collecting items for the women's shelter. I'm the responsible one, the one who sweats the small stuff. I'm the Type A personality everybody avoids until they need me.

Sitting down, I tap it out quick: dates, location, goals, driving times, more information at the next youth group meeting. I add a reminder that everything for the women's shelter has to be collected by the first of next month. Sending it out, I go back to chapter seventeen of Matthew. Before they find the piece of money in the fish's mouth, Jesus casts a devil out of an insane boy, then scolds His disciples for not having the faith to save the boy themselves.

If ye have faith as a grain of mustard seed, ye shall say unto this mountain, Remove hence to yonder place; and it shall remove; and nothing shall be impossible unto you. Holly, is that why you used a fish to deliver your message? To lead me to this passage and warn me that I've lost the faith to save anybody?

Or maybe I really am going crazy, and this is… no, no! The catfish was real; Tyler saw it too. The ring is real. All of this is happening.

I kneel down, resting my elbows on the seat of my desk chair. *Holy God, in Jesus's name, I pray. Help us. Give me some sign. I don't know how or why any of this is happening, but I know that You are good and infinitely merciful. I know that You will never abandon us…*

No. I don't know any of that anymore.

Want to hear something I never told you, Holly?

It was after your me-maw got really sick, when we were waiting at the hospital. Remember the too-bright halls always bustling, even late at night? Sometimes it was actually fun—exploring everywhere and playing tag up and down and across the elevator bank. Remember the corner of the lobby we'd staked out, watching people and talking and laughing until our faces hurt?

But that whole time, I felt like there was something I needed to do. Something I'd forgotten kept wiggling at the base of my brain. I thought and thought, but I couldn't figure out what. So I followed you around like a puppy. Whenever any little chore came up—running to the Chevron for snacks and toothbrushes, going to find the nurse—I jumped to it. But no matter what, God kept prodding me, prodding me. There was something else He expected me to do.

I remember you were braiding my hair when your pa-paw found us in the lobby. He hadn't left her room for three days, and when we saw him, we knew. Knowing couldn't cushion the blow. All our waiting couldn't make us ready.

Your pa-paw held you while you both cried, and I sat watching, one sneaker pressing down on the other. I prayed for God to tell me what to do. Fingers digging into the chair's slick vinyl, I prayed to take some of your pain on my shoulders, one pebble from the heap. I was furious because God refused.

I didn't know what I was asking, Holly. Now you're gone, gone, gone, and I know the Lord refused my prayer because I couldn't have handled it. One pebble would have crushed me.

While your pa-paw talked to the funeral home, you squeezed my hand—I can still almost feel your fingers in mine—and asked me to spend the night with you. Of course I said yes to camping out on your floor in clothes I'd worn for two days.

The next morning, your pa-paw fixed sausage and eggs and said we were going to Robbins' Music.

Your mouth was full of biscuit when you asked, "You're getting a new guitar?"

He shook his head. "It's for you, Little Bit. If you'll play it at your me-maw's service."

"What song?"

"Don't think she'll care."

The guitar you picked was cream and chrome, so pretty I hated to touch it and get fingerprints on it. You decided to play "I Know Who Holds Tomorrow," digging the song out of the big suitcase where your pa-paw kept his sheet music. It was a good choice, Holly, but remember trying to learn it? You'd been playing your pa-paw's guitars for years by then. Picking up songs was as easy for you as picking wildflowers; I'd seen you work out a song after three or four listens. But that day, for whatever reason, you wrestled with it. You had to rip the tune out of the strings. The new electric guitar wouldn't play right. It didn't feel like your pa-paw's black thumping acoustic. You fiddled with the knobs and chords, but nothing helped.

I sat cross-legged on your bed while the night drew down. God pushing me to do something. He needed me to *tell* you something, but I didn't know what.

Then the melody tore in your hands again. You grabbed the guitar's neck like you wanted to strangle it.

"Come on, Holly. You can do this." Hollow words clanged like empty gas cans.

"No, I can't."

"Just relax, stop getting upset, and—"

"Jane, shut up, okay? This guitar's messed up. The pick-ups aren't right or something."

"I don't think it's messed up. Let's just take a break—"

"It's messed up, okay? I can't do this! I can't!" You swung the guitar up, ready to smash it. I caught your wrists before I even realized I'd jumped off the bed.

"Stop! It's not messed up. It's new. It's new, and ... and you're scared. You're just scared of it." It sounded like gibberish, even to me, but somehow I knew it was what I needed to say. "How are you going to stop being scared of it?"

"Jane—"

"How are you going to be fearless, Holly? Because you have to. You have to be." God held both of us, Holly. I felt Him. The days of waiting, of standing by being useless, it was so I could be with you right then, telling you to be fearless.

We walked out to the garage in that cool red hour before nightfall, when fireflies flash and every tree, bird, and blade of grass seems enchanted, when you can't help but see it all, really *see* it. Scrounging through the tools and boxes of scrap wood, we found stencils and spray paint. You glorified the guitar's white base in sunrise crimson: *FEAR NOT.*

At the funeral, your lonely guitar sounded thin under the steepled roof, but the song never broke or stumbled. You were fearless, beautiful and fearless.

Then what? A week later? Gail Bailey invited you to join the praise band. Eleven with chewed fingernails, or fifteen and gorgeous, I watched you yank grown men to their feet with your music. You could make them sing and dance and cry.

God's love used to surround us, Holly. When I prayed,

I felt it fill my chest, swelling until it burst up in tea kettle shouts. And the more I shouted the more it swelled inside me. Holly, it was nearly too much to handle sometimes.

But then you died, and God ran away. He's gone, and I don't know why. I kneel and bow my head and say the words, but they can't open my heart anymore. My heart is broken and useless like an old watch. It's a lump of rusted-up metal in my chest. All I do is kneel here and talk to you.

You remember those evenings when we had the run of downtown, Holly? After youth group, walking over to Court Street to get coffee or whatever, but mostly just burning to rush around and be loud and be alive? Sometimes I'd glance up past the lampposts, and there was no sky. The moon was dark. City lights blotted out the stars. I'd look up into dead black forever.

That's what it feels like since you disappeared. I shut my eyes and whisper praise. I grovel, I threaten, but none of it matters. God stole my best friend, then left me in the darkness. That's what it feels like deep down in my belly. Deep, deep down where I'm afraid to look. *O Lord, how long shall I cry, and thou will not hear? Even cry out unto thee of violence, and thou wilt not save!*

But five barn swallows are sold for two farthings, and not one of them is forgotten by God. How could I spend hours praying and not sense one glimmer of Him?

Last Tuesday, I decided it must be a test. God couldn't really leave me; it was a test of faith. I knelt here for hours, Holly, not getting up for a sip of water, praying until my tongue got gummy and stuck to my teeth. Praying while the carpet chewed my knees raw, then offering the pain up as a sign of devotion. Tim was just worried about me, but when he wouldn't leave me alone, I threatened to throw him down the stairs.

That's when Dad called Dr. Haq, the psychiatrist. I told him I hadn't been sleeping. I promised him and my parents I'd keep it together. But I couldn't tell them I don't feel God anymore, that whenever I close my eyes, it feels like I'm alone in ten billion miles of darkness. They would assure me that God will never give me more than I can handle. They'd make it seem like I'd given up on Him, not the other way around.

A knock on the door makes me jump. "Jane! Dinner."

"I'm asleep. Go away."

Tim leaves without another word. After a while, I hear Faye's birdsong laugh from the kitchen. I've worn their patience down to a sullen nub. They cried at your funeral, and they were there for me afterward, but they're exhausted now. They want everything to go back to normal. They want me to get back to normal and stop scaring them.

I try my best, Holly. Dr. Haq gave me a prescription for Tenex to help me sleep. I take my pill every night and show everybody a smiling face, just some days are harder than others. I miss you. Without you, I don't have anybody to talk to about this stuff anymore.

Fear not, fear not, fear not. God commands His followers to "fear not" 365 times throughout the Old and New Testaments, once for every day of the year. Sitting cross-legged on the carpet, I flip through my Bible. My fingers find those words, your creed, again and again.

Fear not, for I am with thee…

Say to them that are of a fearful heart, Be strong, fear not…

I whisper the verses, tasting the dry papery words on my tongue and lips. Please, let them change me, make me as faithful as you were. But they're just words; they aren't real anymore.

Be strong and of a good courage, fear not, nor be afraid of them: for the LORD thy God, He it is that doth go with thee; He will not fail thee, nor forsake thee.

I throw the Bible. It hits the wall, falling splayed like a dead swallow. The violence feels good.

Then I feel guilty, then ashamed, then scared. I grab the Bible again, smoothing out the bent pages. Setting it on the bed, I fold to the floor, hiding my face in my hands. I want to cry, but I can't anymore. I cried and cried for weeks, then my tears just ran out. I'm nothing but stomach acid and too-tight skin anymore.

Sadness swells in my chest but can't escape. I try to force a sob, push it out, but it doesn't work. I can't cry, I can't pray. I feel like a dead, dried-up fly on the windowsill.

Holly, how did you watch cancer eat your me-maw's bones and still love God? How did you still feel His love for you? I'm an idiot, Holly, and I'm sorry. I really thought a few kind words and spray-painting your guitar were all you needed to cheer you up. I didn't know anything could hurt this bad.

And your parents. Everybody says it's a miracle you lived. They'd offer praise unto the Highest when they heard your story.

But sometimes you'd get sad for no reason. Those days,

you'd try to tell me how it really felt, dangling in the flipped-over car with your parents' torn bodies. You could only talk in a hoarse whisper that first day I met you because you'd lost your voice in that car. You screamed for your mom over and over, but she never answered.

I'm sorry, Holly. You would talk about the sticky blood and smashed glass and the smell of gasoline, and I'd try to change the subject. I'd yammer about clothes, bands, or boys, nothing that mattered, nothing that couldn't be snatched away in an instant. I thought I was being a good friend, helping you take your mind off of it. I'm so sorry, sorry, sorry.

I should have washed your feet, Holly. I should have begged you to tell me how you could still be so beautiful, still bring so much beauty into the world. I had a million chances to ask, and I squandered every one.

I loved you, Holly, but I didn't know how much I needed you. I know now. I'm ready to listen. Please, Holly, tell me how to open my heart again.

Five

The carpet is hot and scratchy like a rash. I rub my eyes open. Sweat slicks my face and makes my church dress cling to my thighs. I stare up at the bed as fragments of dream chase me into waking.

I dreamed I was back in your house, but black lake-bottom mud had flooded it. The stuff sucked off one of my shoes. It caked my calves and hands and clumped in my hair. Holly, you were under there somewhere, coughed up from the drowned forest with the mud. Other bodies too, old tires, busted Mountain Dew bottles. And I knew—the certainty made me want to vomit—that no matter how carefully I walked, eventually I'd step on a cold hand or ankle.

I try to make myself cry again. I snuffle and sniff, but no tears come. The sadness never unwinds from the tight little knot in my breast.

It's 11:51. I pull off my sweat-sticky dress and crawl into bed. My brain's already woken up, though. Thoughts squawk and wheel around like barn swallows. I'll lie here all night if I don't take my medicine.

As I slip down to the kitchen, my feet probe for the stairs in the dark. This will always be strange to me, how quiet the house is at midnight, the daylight free-for-all fading to almost nothing. It gets so quiet I can hear the clunk of the air conditioner turning on. When we first moved into this house, the mechanical noises deep inside the walls scared me. Dad told me they were house elves. They watched over us at night, making sure we were always safe. I slept soundly curled up in the lie.

Blood drops have been wiped off the kitchen counter. The knife, already cleaned, sits in the dishwasher. I fill a glass with water and swallow two of the scab-pink Tenex. The stuff poisons time. It makes nights wither away. I won't remember falling asleep or waking up. It'll just suddenly be bright morning. I won't have any dreams.

Mom left a cling-wrapped plate of spaghetti for me in the fridge. I eat a cold meatball with my fingers. I poke through the salad for tomato wedges and slices of cucumber. Your pa-paw, he's moved close to the river, hasn't he?

The thought lands as lightly as a bird on a twig. I freeze, afraid of startling it.

Your pa-paw couldn't live in that house by himself—I was afraid to just visit, how could he live there by himself? But still, the river seeps into his thoughts just like it seeps into my dreams. Just like it seeped into Tyler's mind when he wrote that lonely song. The drowned forest holds us all tight. If your pa-paw hasn't run far away from it—and he hasn't because we saw him at Rivercall—then he's moved as close to the water as he can. As close as he can to you, Holly.

Yes, yes, yes! I flap my hands like Yuri.

It's not much, but it's a place to start looking. I'll call Tyler first thing in the morning. We're coming, Holly. We're going to save you.

Six

The light stings.

Mom talks through the door.

It's 10:19.

I need to call Tyler; we should already be gone.

"Jane!"

"Wha . . . ?" I shift, stare at the closed door. "What?"

"Bo Greene is here," Mom repeats. "Get up, Jane. Come downstairs."

Why is Bo here? Then my heart thumps hard. Oh no, no, Holly, no. Did Pastor Wesley send him?

I kick the covers off and get up. The dresser drawer slips its track when I yank it open, almost hitting my foot. I spit angry words and grab some jean shorts from the mess, leaving the rest on the floor.

Dang it, we should be looking for your pa-paw by now! I set my alarm, but I must have slept through it. It's the Tenex,

Holly. I sleepwalk. Dad swears I've had whole conversations with him I don't remember.

In the bathroom, I brush my teeth while stepping into my Yellow Box sandals, then wrangle my hair into a ponytail. Maybe it's not about your ring. Maybe Mom called Bo because of the fight I had with her last night.

I head downstairs. I have to tell them how sorry I am. And remember to smile. Just smile, sprinkle them with a little sugar, and don't argue about anything. As long as they let me leave with Tyler today, that's the only important thing.

On the living room floor, Yuri plays with his Legos, building them up into a tilting tower. Bo sits on the couch, and Mom talks to him softly. Dad hovers nearby. It confuses me why he's not at work, but then I remember it's Labor Day.

When they see me, Mom goes quiet. Bo stands up grinning. "Hey there, Jane. Sorry about waking you up for all this."

"It's okay." What does he mean by "all this"?

"How's it going?"

"Pretty good."

Bo sits down at the end of the couch now, so I can sit between him and Mom. Close up, he smells like Hugo Boss mixed with dust and cut grass.

"So ... what's up?" I ask.

"Well, Pastor Wesley wanted me to stop by."

"Oh."

"You and Tyler talked to him yesterday. And you said some things that ... worried him."

"Oh." My lips are suddenly dry, sticking to my gums.

Dad asks, "Honey, what's this about a ring? About Holly's ring?"

"Some—" I lick my lips. I have to make them hear the truth. *Please Lord, let them hear the truth.* "Something happened at Rivercall, with that catfish. It had Holly's promise ring in its mouth. She wrote *HELP* across it. She's trapped in the forest at the bottom of the lake and ... listen! Please, we have to help Holly!"

Mom squeezes my hand. "Honey, no. Holly had an accident. She's at peace now. She's not—Yuri, not now. Let us talk." Yuri wants to show her his Lego tower. She turns him away, turns back to me. "Holly's in Heaven with her mom and dad. She's not trapped—"

"I know it sounds crazy, but it's the truth." If I could show them the ring, maybe they'd believe me, but Tyler has it. Stupid, stupid—why didn't I keep it? "The catfish ... hold on." I get up to get my Bible, but Mom grabs my arm.

"Jane, please."

"Listen, listen. In Matthew 17, the apostles find a coin inside a fish's mouth, just like we found Holly's ring. See? And in that same chapter, Jesus tells them they—"

Crow's feet crinkle around her eyes. I'm making her old.

"Jane, I'm going to call Dr. Haq," Dad says. "We're going to get you some help, okay?"

"No! Listen! I'm trying to explain to you, but you won't listen. I can't talk to Dr. Haq. I have stuff to do."

"What stuff?"

I hesitate. "Just stuff, okay? I just have to go, okay?"

"Jane, no. You're not going anywhere," Mom says.

"Mom, please, I...I'm sorry about the fight, but I can't talk to Dr. Haq right now. Please. I'm sorry."

"No, no, no..." She pulls me close, holds me against her heartbeat like a baby. "This isn't punishment. I'm not mad about the fight. Nobody's mad, nobody's mad."

I've put her through so much. I start to sob. "I didn't mean to hurt you. It was an accident. I'm sorry—"

"Just help you move on. Just so I get my angel back—"

"Sorry I got mad. I love you, okay? I love you."

"We should pray. Let's pray." Bo gently pries my fingers from Mom's arm. "Hey, Yuri? Yuri, can you come here?"

Yuri's fingers lie in mine, soft and slightly damp. Mom still has one arm around me. Her other hand clutches Dad's hand, which grasps Bo's. I'm sniffling. So is Mom. We shut our eyes and bow our heads to the darkness.

Bo leads us. "Dear Lord, we ask you to watch over Jane. And watch over all of us, Lord. We place ourselves in your care. Lord, give us the wisdom and courage to do what's right, even when it's hard. Help us find the path, Lord. Your path."

Why won't God help me this one tiny bit? I put my family through so much—I'm a terrible kid—but I have to put them through some more.

While Bo asks His blessing, I open my eyes. Whipping my hand free, I twist Yuri's ear. He jerks back, but I hold on, twisting harder. He bellows and takes a swing. I dodge. Bo catches a meaty smack in the mouth. "We pray—ow!"

Mom goes to calm Yuri down. Wailing, cupping his hurt ear, Yuri punches her in the chest. Dad pulls Bo back,

49

stumbling. Bo bit his tongue when Yuri hit him, and blood stains his teeth pink.

I take the stairs two at a time. Faye and Tim watch from the top.

"What happened?"

"Just stay here."

My pulse beats against my temples so hard it hurts, but my thoughts run smooth. Ducking into my room, I grab my phone from the dresser. The twenty-dollar bill Mom gave me yesterday lies folded up underneath. I meant to give it back to her since Tyler and I never got any coffee. Grabbing it, I stuff it in my front pocket, just in case.

Back into the hall, back past Faye and Tim, back downstairs. Mom has the afghan around Yuri's shoulders. He moans, rocking back and forth. Dad is apologizing to Bo, who's holding a paper towel to his split lip. Nobody notices as I step out the kitchen door.

I cut through backyards and Mrs. Peterson's flower garden. Colored-glass witch balls watch me pass. I shove, tug, and stomp through the windbreak of lilac and plum, then cut catty-corner across the cotton field on the other side. Each step breaks the dry crust of topsoil, my feet sinking into darker, moist earth. My calves brush through the rows of plants, making them whisper to one another as I pass.

Tyler answers his phone while eating something. "Hey, w'sup?"

"Is everything okay?"

"Yeah. Why wouldn't—?"

"Bo hasn't been by your house yet?"

"Nuh-uh." He swallows. "What's going on?"

"Bo came to my house. He told Mom about the ring, about everything."

"Oh no."

"But listen, I think I might know where Mr. Alton is. Sorta. But we have to go *now*. Come pick me up at the Texaco on Reservation Road."

"Okay. I'm coming. I'm looking for my keys now."

"Hurry. But be careful. But hurry. And bring the ring."

I slip my phone into my purse. In the heat-shimmering distance, a tractor pulls a sprayer across the dusty cotton plants. Their leaves are withered brown, and their bolls are fixing to split open. Some already have, revealing the clean whiteness inside. The farmer watches me crossing his field without a wave or nod.

There's a dull pain in my solar plexus. I force some deep breaths and let myself feel bad for hurting Yuri, for making him hurt Bo and Mom. I'm in trouble. I don't even know what Mom and Dad will do now. But I promised I was coming, Holly. Me and Tyler will find your pa-paw and figure out what's going on and how we can help you. We're coming.

I plod along the field, then quick-step it across four lanes of hot asphalt to the gas station. If I'd known I was running away from home today, I wouldn't have worn flip-flops.

Seven

"Okay. So you had a dream about Mr. Alton, and he was down somewhere by the river?"

"I don't...I mean..." The dream has fled. It seemed so vivid when I woke up, but now all I can remember is the impression it left, like following deer tracks in mud. "It was about the river, but I don't think Mr. Alton was in it."

"Why are we doing this, then?" Tyler's voice is full of vinegar.

I snap back, "Because you don't have any better ideas."

So we drive past the condos lining the downtown embankments, eyes squinted, searching for your pa-paw's old pickup. We search Tuck's Cove, that harbor east of the Indian mound. Tyler doesn't say a word. He's worried about what Bo is telling his parents right now. He's annoyed with me, thinking we're wasting time.

But your pa-paw has come to the river, Holly. I know this because it's what draws our dreams and deepest thoughts. He's come to the river because everything else is so thin. The stupid stuff people talk about—what they ate for lunch, some sale at Foot Locker—I get mad just listening to them now. The river is the only thing that feels real anymore.

But Wilson Lake is fifteen hundred acres. Half a dozen marinas dot its shores. Probably two dozen resorts and campgrounds, and hundreds of cabins on private land. This could take forever.

Pulling out of Tuck's Cove, Tyler says, "Well, where to next?"

"There's Bay Hill Marina, the one with the restaurant."

"On the south shore?" He groans.

"We can't give up until we've looked everywhere."

"Yeah, yeah," Tyler sighs. "Let me make a stop first."

"What? What do you have to do now?"

"A friend is leaving town. I need to say goodbye."

"We don't have—"

"It'll take five minutes, Jane."

I slump down in the seat. "Five minutes, right?"

"Five minutes."

Neither of us say anything else. My phone rings. Mom again, and this time I turn it off. Your pa-paw's down by the shore, Holly. I know because he has to be. Please, God, let him be. Otherwise, we're totally lost.

We drive to a neighborhood that was probably really pretty once. Now it's falling apart. Porches sag, and tinfoil covers windows. Tree roots tilt the sidewalk slabs until they crack. There's a lawn that's all weeds and tire ruts, with a white Florence Utilities van parked under a maple. Ultimate Steve sits on the front porch with a bunch of people I don't know. They're all older. They're all as shabby-looking as the house.

I follow Tyler through the front gate. It looks like somebody bashed in the mailbox with a baseball bat, then scribbled *Shut up! You can't play!!!* across it with paint marker. There's a girl on the porch wearing Jackie O sunglasses, her black-soled feet propped on the railing. Launching a jet of cigarette smoke, she yells, "Whoo, Tyler! Show us some tits!"

The rest of them fall out laughing. We've walked into the tail end of a running joke. Judging from the empty beer bottles and overflowing ashtrays, it's been running since last night.

Tyler grins. "Morning, LeighAnn."

The girl stands up, blocking our way. "Do it!" she answers. "Tits!"

And he does. Like a puppy performing a trick, Tyler yanks the front of his shirt up, showing a soft slab of belly and chest.

"That's what momma likes," she crows, stepping aside. "That's it!"

"Max, can't you do anything with her?" Tyler asks the guy picking at a guitar.

"I've tried. Believe me, I have tried."

Ultimate Steve gives Tyler that shoulder-banging half-hug boys do. "Missed all the fun! Thought you were coming after that church thing yesterday." He scratches at his beard like he's got fleas. I can't help glancing at the stump of his missing pinky finger. Idiot.

"I was. Just, uh…some stuff came up after. Just didn't feel like a party."

"Holly stuff?" LeighAnn asks. When Tyler nods, they all sort of lean toward him for a moment. LeighAnn wraps an arm around his neck, presses her head against his.

Who are these people?

"But hey, I couldn't let Patterson run off." Stepping around LeighAnn, Tyler gives the tall guy a real hug, squeezing him tight. "Glad I didn't miss you."

"Me too." Really tall, Patterson stands stooped over everybody else, like a tree in a storm. "Hey, I'm giving you my Vox."

"What? Why?"

Patterson shrugs. "I won't have the space for it. But we took off the casters, so you'll have to find new ones."

"Well, thanks. Really. But doesn't the band need—"

LeighAnn shakes her head. "We've got the Mini Colossals with the Weber speakers."

"That Vox is de-damn-licious, though," Max adds. "Shut up and take it."

They talk about push-pulls and SPSs and two-by-twelves. It's white noise to me, but ends with Tyler following Patterson into the house to grab the amplifier. Through the door, I glimpse the living room—a drum kit beside the couch, and walls covered in stained burgundy carpet. Somebody's sleeping on the couch with his arm thrown over his eyes. I waffle, not sure if I should follow them in or not. Then the storm door bangs shut and I'm stuck outside.

"Jane? How goes it?" Ultimate Steve asks.

"Good."

He nods, shaking a cigarette from a half-empty pack. A girl with a sketchy-looking dye job sits on the porch rail, talking to LeighAnn. When Steve leans back, she wraps her arms and legs around him. He turns to whisper some little joke to her. She chuckles, nuzzling his ear. She's gross. I can see her pink satin whale-tail sticking out of the back of her shorts.

"So this was, like, a goodbye party?" I ask.

"Uh-huh. Yeah. Patterson just finished his bachelor's in forestry . . . " LeighAnn gets distracted searching for a lighter. "Uh, headed up to South Carolina. To the Congaree National Park."

"Neat. So he's going to be a park ranger?"

"Yeah, but actually, natural resources manager."

"Okay. Neat." I nod without really knowing what that means.

"Yeah."

We fall into foot-shuffling silence. Empty beer bottles fill the window sill behind Max. Draining another one, he sets it in the line.

"Want something to drink?" LeighAnn asks.

"What? No."

Ultimate Steve laughs. "Jane's church-folk, LeighAnn."

"I meant a Mountain Dew or something." She curls her lip at him. "I figured she's—you're still in high school, right?"

"I'm fifteen."

"Yeah, so I wasn't going to give her beer, just that it's miserable hot out here." She turns back to me. "So, want some sweet tea? Or we've got just water or—"

"I'm not thirsty, but thank you."

LeighAnn nods. "And just for, whatever, the record? This

is kind of a special occasion, with Patterson leaving and Labor Day and all. We're usually sober by Monday morning."

They all laugh. Max says, "Now, don't *lie* to the girl, Lee-Lee."

"I'm not! I don't know about you, but I don't—"

"What about Fourth of July? When we went to your brother's?"

"That was a special occasion too! That was celebrating the birth of our country!"

"What about when Twitchy was here?"

"Twitchy was here! Another special occasion!" Now LeighAnn's laughing along with them. "I can't help it if my life is blessed with good friends and cheap beer."

They all think it's hilarious. I just stand there, silent, while they jabber like blue jays. I notice that LeighAnn, Max, and Ultimate Steve all have the same tattoo—the silhouette of an airplane—inked onto their inner right forearms. When Tyler and Patterson reappear, carrying a battered black amp between them, I see that Patterson has the same tattoo. I guess it means they're in a band together, or maybe a cult.

Tyler and Patterson load the amp into the rear of Tyler's pickup, then come back to lean against the porch railing. Tyler asks, "Ultimate, you spending the night in South Carolina?"

Ultimate Steve shakes his head. "Have to be at work tomorrow. Dropping Patterson off and turning right around."

Max says, "Don't even slow down, just open the door and shove him out," but nobody's listening.

Tyler asks, "How many days have you been up?"

Steve shrugs.

"Tyler, we need to go," I say.

"What? You guys running off already?" Steve asks. "Come on, big guy."

"Sorry, but yeah. We've got some … uh, stuff that can't wait. But listen, nobody's called looking for me, have they?"

"No. Should I be expecting someone?"

"Well, just in case my parents call? Tell them I've been with you all day, but I just left. Okay?"

"Sure." The way Ultimate Steve grins at me when he says it is the last straw. Snatching Tyler's keys out of his hand, I hiss in his ear. "You want to hang out here all day? Fine. Maybe one of the herpes sponges over there'll make out with you. I'm going to help Holly."

I walk off the porch. None of them are worth a glance backward. Tyler yells after me, "Okay! We'll go, Jane. Give me one second, okay?"

I should leave him, Holly. Instead, I slide into the passenger seat and wait for him to say his goodbyes. Steve follows him down to the pickup. "Sometime soon, you need to get with Max. Patterson's leaving, and we need a rhythm guitar, and—"

Tyler shakes his head as he climbs in. "Thanks, but I've just got a lot going on right now."

"Come on." Setting his hands above the door, Steve shakes the truck on its chassis. "What's more important than *rock*?"

"I've just got a lot going on right now."

"Well, think about it at least."

"I'll think about it. See you around."

"See you."

They bump fists through the window. Steve doesn't say anything to me. Did he hear what I told Tyler? I don't care if he did or not—him or any of those other losers.

Tyler pulls away from the curb, slipping his Aviators on. "What was that about?"

"You tell me."

"Tell you what?"

"Well, when did you start hanging out with Ultimate Steve again, anyway?"

"He called me after Holly's accident, and, whatever, we started hanging out."

"So that's where you've been the past month? Getting drunk with Steve and his band? Hiding in that house back there?"

"Did you see me drinking?"

I stare out the window.

"Did you see me drinking?"

"No."

"Then don't accuse me of stuff. I said goodbye to a guy I'll probably never see again. You should get that; you of all people."

"Fine. I do. But then why don't you come to church anymore?"

"Oh, come on," he groans. "Jane, don't go all Jesus dork on me, okay? I can't deal with it right now."

"Our faith is being tested, Tyler, and we're failing! If you'd been coming to church, maybe God would show us where to find Holly's pa-paw now." I touch Tyler's wrist. "Maybe if you promised to start coming again. If you were sincere, maybe He would—"

Tyler yanks his hand away. "Maybe if you'd visited Mr. Alton once since Holly drowned, you'd already know where he is. Maybe we wouldn't need a miracle then."

"I ... I'm not pretending to be perfect, Tyler."

"Good, because you're not, so stop dumping it all on me."

We head across the dam to the south shore and Bay Hill Marina. I stare at my hands folded in my lap.

"Tyler, we're going up against ... I don't even know. But we're going to need gifts of the spirit. This is a time of trial for us, and we need the gift of wisdom to see truth from lies."

"This isn't a 'time of trial,' Jane. It's just crazy shit that's happening."

"Tyler!"

"It's crazy, fucked-up shit, and talking in Sunday sermons won't help."

"Tyler, I—"

"You want to know why I haven't been going to church? Because I never got anything out of it, okay? Not really. I liked spending time with Holly. That's all."

"That's a lie!"

"It's not! I was never seized by the Holy Spirit or whatever. Like God was showing me things or whatever. Now that Holly's gone, there's no reason to go anymore."

It's a lie, Holly, I know it is. We saw him filled with the Holy Fire. We saw the tears on his cheeks when he was saved. But now Tyler is hurting and angry and falling away from the

Lord's embrace. I want to help, I want to say the right thing, but I'm pathetic at that stuff. You know I am.

You were the one who loved everybody and made them feel loved. You're the one they all leaned toward like plants toward the sun. You're the one who should be here. But I try to imagine what you would tell Tyler right now.

A question. You wouldn't *tell* him anything, you'd ask a question.

"So ... what's their name?"

"What?" Tyler's voice is thin and tight like a wire. He thinks I want to argue some more.

"Steve and his friends. They're a band, right? What's their band name?"

"Stratofortress."

"Huh?"

"Strat-o-fortress. It's a kind of plane."

I nod. "So why'd they name themselves that?"

"Don't know, I wasn't there."

I look back down at my hands. "Well, at least it's better than that other band name."

"What other band name?"

"The name of the band you and Ultimate Steve were in."

"Was I ever in a band with Steve?"

"Yes, you—" He almost got me, Holly. Then I see the grin cracking through his mask of confusion. "You're not making me say it."

"Say what?"

"The name of the band."

"Why?"

"Because it's stupid."

"I was never in a band called 'Stupid.' I'd remember that."

"No, not—I'm not saying it."

"Well, you're the one who keeps bringing it up."

"Well, I'm the one who's dropping it."

"Dropping what?"

I stare out the window.

"Dropping what?"

"Ahghh. You're like my brother."

"Dropping what?"

"The band," I say, hiding my face in my hands now.

"Which band?"

"Quit!"

"A band called 'Quit'? I kinda like that. Very art rock. Very—"

"Tighty-Whitey and the Banana Hammocks!"

And when I shout the name, you're shouting it too, Holly, out in that frost-silvered night on the edge of memory.

"That's disgusting," I'd said.

"Don't be like that. This is going to be fun." Under the street lamps, your eyes shimmered. Your cheeks glowed pink from the cold. Fingers around my wrist, you pulled me up the sidewalk into the bowling alley.

They were some of your school friends. I only knew Tyler, who'd come to youth group with you the week before. I didn't like him. Two years older than us, big and loud, already a rock star in his own mind. He was—he is—the kind of guy who'd think a band name like that was hilarious.

You didn't tell me their show was a rock opera, Holly.

Or that one of their buddies would run up wearing a rubber dragon mask—but somehow representing their gym coach—and put Jeb White in a chicken-wing armlock. Or that, defeated and stripped to his underwear, Jeb would sing a song rhyming "loneliness and fear" with "Buzz Lightyear." Or that finally he would battle with the dragon again, this time wielding the unstoppable power of rock 'n' roll.

I stood in the bowling alley snack bar, in an audience of nine people (including Steve's mom), thinking this was what drugs must feel like. But you bounced around and pumped your fist. Bending your mouth to my ear, you yelled, "They're pretty awesome, huh?"

They were ridiculous, Holly. You could have played better with your feet. Your cheeks still glowed pink, though, even out of the cold. When you looked at Tyler, your eyes still shimmered.

I asked, "You like him?"

"No. But kinda." You buried your face against my shoulder. "But really I just wanted to support him. He quit the marching band this year so he could focus on his real music."

"I was just gonna say he plays guitar like a guy who's spent years practicing the tuba."

"Jane, don't be like that."

"Like what?"

"Like you always are."

Jeb decided not to slay the dragon—that's not what the power of rock 'n' roll was for. Instead they shared Pixy Stix and closed the show with a duet of "Bridge Over Troubled Water."

"So does he like you?" I asked, as they sang against the thunder of bowling balls.

"I don't know. I mean, yeah, but there's this other girl he really likes. Amber."

"But what? She didn't come tonight?"

"She's not into music like this."

"Forget Amber, then." And what else could I do but jump up into one of the booth seats? "Whoo! Banana Hammocks! Yeah!"

The band looked over, a little startled. Steve's mom looked over.

"Encore! Banana Hammocks! Hit me again!" Then you joined in. "Tyler! Banana Hammocks! Yay, Tyler!"

The band grabbed their instruments again. They started into something sharp, fast, and just barely holding itself together—the musical equivalent of getting shoved down the stairs. You loved it. You jumped around and hugged my neck.

I yelled into your ear, "If he's still thinking about Amber after this, we'll kidnap him and you can have your way with him, yeah?"

"Cool! Can I keep him tied up in your garage?"

"Sure!"

Now, without you, Tyler and me chuckle together, even though I'm mad at him.

"No, you were so into us," he says. "You were more into us than Holly."

"What? Whatever. I only made a total fool of myself hoping you'd get up the guts to ask Holly out. You're welcome, by the way."

"Don't lie. We had you revved up."

"Whatever. I just knew if Holly paid seven dollars to wear ugly bowling shoes and listen to that, she really loved you."

The word sucks all the air out of the car. Death rots the sweetest memories first, Holly. It hides inside them like a razor blade in an apple.

But you did love him, didn't you? Even though he was loud-mouthed and filthy-minded, you loved him, and God used your love to draw Tyler to the church. We saw the bigger-than-life rock star choke up and tremble the night he was saved.

I judge people too quickly, Holly, I know. I'm prickly, I don't give them a chance, Jesus doesn't want me for a sunbeam, I know, I know. But you know what? Happy little sunbeams don't rescue their friends' trapped souls from rivers. The sunbeams—Hanna Marie, Brooke, all of them—they cried for a few days, then moved on. They're out goofing off and making out with boys. I'm all you've got left.

They could move on because they don't still need you, Holly. But who's going to keep me from being prickly and judgmental all the time now? Did you even think about that before you went and drowned?

I chew my thumbnail, peeling it away from the stinging quick. Fine, fine, I'll try to be nicer. I'll try to be more open. For you.

Along the highway, the sun flashes through the tops of the pines like a school of fish. Then there's the sign: *Bay Hill Marina & Resort*. Tyler turns in, steering past the fuel dock and floating restaurant.

"That's his truck! There." He jabs me in the shoulder. "You were right. You figured it out."

"We don't know if he knows anything about Holly. We haven't figured anything out yet." Still, I clasp my hands together for a quick prayer of thanks.

Tyler pulls into the spot beside your pa-paw's pickup. Down the steep slope, the marina fans out across the water. Boats idle in and out, sending brown diesel clouds scudding across the water. Shirtless, lobster-skinned men yell back and forth, cluttering the docks with coolers, tackle boxes, coiled hoses, radios. Everything is covered in spiderwebs and bird poop.

And there's that smell, the fetid stink of lake-bottom mud. It's the smell of afternoons on Dad's boat. Of swimming lessons. Of thrashing, glittering bass pulled from the water. It's the smell the monster catfish carried up with it too. It's the smell of Swallow's Nest Bluff and the day you drowned. And it's really the smell of death, isn't it? It's fish and plants rotting to black slime down in the drowned forest.

"There he is," Tyler says, making me whirl around. "Mr. Alton! Hey!"

He's lying on the dock, skinny butt in the air, beside a houseboat that needs a paint job. Seeing us, he climbs to his feet, pulling a fistful of weeds out of the water in one hand, a steak knife in the other. "Well, hey, Tyler. How are you? And Jane too." He shoves the dripping mass of plants into a Taco Bell bag already fat with hacked-up stalks. Starting to hug me, he stops because his arms are wet. I hug him instead.

"How've you been, Little Bit?" he whispers.

I don't know how to answer, so I squeeze him tighter. He's thin, Holly. I can feel his ribs.

"What's all that?" Tyler asks, pointing to the bag.

"Oh, this milfoil is terrible." He drops the bag on the houseboat's deck. Boats on this side of the marina move through thousands of feathery stalks poking out of the water. In some spots, the milfoil has turned the marina into a lawn so lush my dad would kill for it. "It gets tangled in the propellers, gets everywhere. But anyway, can you guys stay? Come aboard, come aboard."

He offers a hand to help me onto the boat. I ask, "So, when'd you buy a boat?"

"Oh, it belongs to a friend. I'm just borrowing it for a while. Staying at the house was just … hard. I just needed to get away for a while."

I nod. I can't imagine what it would be like living there, alone with the silence.

We duck into the cabin, which smells like fast food grease. The houseboat's furniture is scratched and patched, and there's a gap under the counter where the mini-fridge used to be. The only things your pa-paw took from the house are one suitcase, his guitar case, and a bulging photo album. The album is open to some snapshots of your dad and mom and you when you were a toddler, pushing a toy lawn mower.

Tyler pulls himself into the swivel-mounted chair overlooking the piloting console. "So you doing any fishing while you're out here?" he asks.

"Oh, sure. Caught a two-pound crappie yesterday, just off the dock there." Your pa-paw clears the table, grabbing beer bottles, Taco Bell wrappers, and a plastic fork, balancing them on the teetering stack of garbage rising above the trash can's rim. I slide into the booth. There's more photos, all of your me-maw, lined up along the edge of the table so your pa-paw can stare at them while he's eating. Still talking about the fish he caught, he scoops them up and slips them into the photo album.

He flips to another part of the album, one filled with publicity shots and newspaper clippings. Taking out a picture, he hands it to Tyler. "All right, young man, tell me who that is."

"Duane Allman," Tyler says without hesitation.

Your pa-paw laughs. "You know it."

"But this was before the Allman Brothers, right? Back when he was just a studio musician, right?"

"*Just* a studio musician?"

"I mean—"

"Yeah, Aretha Franklin came in the one week, and Duane *just* wrote her an R&B hit. Then the Osmonds came in the next week, and we *just* knocked out a bubblegum hit for them. Then Jimmy Hughes—"

"How about I *just* keep my mouth shut from now on?" Tyler asks.

Your pa-paw laughs again, handing him another picture. "You don't know this one. You should, but you don't."

"Uh…"

"Give you a hint. Bruce Springsteen and Pins and Needles both did covers of one of his songs."

I know he'll go on forever about FAME Studios and

who he wrote songs for and who he went on tour with. And Tyler will lap up every word.

"Okay, I'll give you another hint," he says.

I cough loudly. "Actually, Mr. Alton, we need to ask you some stuff. About Holly."

He smiles and sighs at the same time. "Should have known you didn't come down just to keep an old fart company."

Was that a joke, or bitterness? Or one disguised as the other? I cringe, staring up at him, not sure if I should laugh or apologize.

"What do you want to know, Little Bit?"

"We wanted to know if any … strange stuff … has happened. Since the accident."

"Strange stuff?"

I look at Tyler, still in the pilot's chair. He gives me a tiny shrug, then tries to help. "Just, y'know, anything strange," he says.

"Okay, Mr. Alton, you know we're not crazy, right? I mean, if we tell you something … "

Your pa-paw's hands are shaking so bad he can't hold the album. Setting it down, he presses them flat against the tabletop. "Her ghost is in the river, isn't it?"

For a moment, there's only the water lapping against the hull. Me and Tyler stare at him, then turn to stare at each other. I say, "Show him the ring."

He presses your ring into your pa-paw's hand. Tyler says, "It's Holly's ring. I gave it to her the day she died."

Turning it between his fingers, your pa-paw sees the word *HELP*. His eyes darken with pain. Tyler tells him about Rivercall and the catfish, about Pastor Wesley saying he wanted to help and Bo showing up at my house.

Your pa-paw closes long, calloused fingers—musician's fingers—around the promise ring. He looks stunned. I don't think he hears half of Tyler's story. Finally, he asks, "But what's happening?"

"We don't know," I say. "That's why we came here. We thought maybe you'd know."

He just shakes his head, and hope evaporates.

"Well, why did you ask if Holly was in the river?"

He bends down and opens his guitar case. Tyler whispers, "The Dreadnought," in a worshipful tone that makes your pa-paw grin weakly.

"Yeah," he mutters, slipping the guitar strap over his head. "Can't go anywhere without her. Only family I've got left."

I cringe again, the joke inch-worming too close to the truth to be funny. But your pa-paw doesn't notice. Carrying the guitar, he leads us up onto the deck.

The old guitar is a C. F. Martin Dreadnought, its glossy black paint scuffed and scratched. It's a veteran of a thousand days in sweltering studios, a thousand nights onstage. He told us he won it from Johnny Cash in a poker game. Of course, he also used to tell us he once had a pet saber-toothed tiger named Gut-Ripper Sam, so who knows.

"Couple nights after I came here, I was playing, and … " He plucks a few notes, stops and tunes one of the strings. "It might not happen this time. I don't know."

"What might not happen?" I ask nervously.

"Just keep your eye on the plants."

He starts playing. Long fingers jump like grease in a hot skillet. The guitar is plain, but it's plain and true. Notes rise from its rosewood chest. A breeze off the river whirls them out across the marina like dandelion seeds.

Under the tea-colored water, streamers of milfoil wave with the currents. I watch them, wiping sweat from my face without looking away.

Hearing the Dreadnought's voice again makes me remember those afternoons when you'd ignore me. I'd try on your clothes or bounce a rubber ball against your floor and closet door, getting so mad that you wouldn't do anything except practice guitar. Sitting on your bed, you'd spend hours curling your fingers at unfamiliar angles across the strings, teaching them to move the way your mind wanted them to.

Tyler lifts his Aviators up, then shakes his head. "What are we—"

I sink fingernails into his arm. "Shhh! Quiet."

I never take my eyes off the weeds. If I don't blink, I can see new spirals of leaves unfolding. Stalks stretch upward, slow as the afternoon shadows, reaching toward the music.

People walk by without noticing, but down in the murk, the milfoil winds around dock bumpers and slack mooring ropes. Tiny snowflake flowers blossom, then fall to the water. The longest stalk reaches under the railing, making me jump back. "Stop! Mr. Alton, stop!"

The song breaks off. The clatter of the marina pours back in on us.

I grip the railing and peer down. "Holly? Holly, where are you?"

There's no sound, no bubbles, no motion in the water except for the plants continuing to grow for several minutes. They keep climbing up the railing, working with the patience of a girl learning her instrument, teaching her fingers to move the way her mind wants them to.

Eight

Your pa-paw stares across the water as he talks. "When I was ten, me and some friends played hooky from school, went swimming in the river. Next day, I got a fever. Bad one, kept me in bed past the end of the school year. Then it got into my liver. After a while my skin turned yellow. My eyes, the whites of them, turned yellow with the jaundice.

"Doctor couldn't help. Everybody thought my liver would shut down completely, and when that happens, that's it. That's the end." He snaps off a stalk of milfoil curled around the railing post. Raking the spiny leaves across his palm, he squints at them, trying to understand.

"I never told my folks I'd skipped school that day, didn't think it mattered. But both my folks grew up down in the holler, the river valley back before they built the dam and flooded it all. Finally, they called a root-worker named Mr. Buckley.

"Root-workers had been pretty common in the holler, back before there were any doctors. Mostly they mixed up medicines, helped lay out the dead, and such. But they knew others things too, charms, curses, and things like that. Mr. Buckley was a little grouchy old man, one of those turtle-faced old men, y'know? He came into my room holding the Bible, looks me up and down, then says, 'What were you up to 'fore you got sick?'

"I told him like I'd told my folks, that I'd just been at school and hadn't been up to nothing. But Mr. Buckley, he holds that Bible out and says, 'You ready to swear to it? Swear to it there on your deathbed?' The word 'deathbed' really scared me, so I told him all about playing hooky. Besides, I figured Dad couldn't whoop me if I was dying." He chuckles.

"So I told them I'd been swimming, and Mr. Buckley nodded, and scratched his chin, and looked around my room, and finally he tells my folks, 'The fever must have followed him home. We gotta find it quick, or it'll do him in.' So they started searching everywhere, under my bed, in the attic. I thought they'd all gone bananas, y'know? Momma even told Dad to pull up the floorboards. He was about to do just that when he noticed the grille over an air duct had been worked loose. He got down and reached in there, started shouting, and pulled out a frog, piss-yellow and this big." He holds up his fist to show us its size. "That was it. That was the fever."

"That *was* the fever?" I ask. "Or, like, the frog gave you germs?"

He shakes his head. "That was the fever. In disguise. Mr. Buckley killed it with a shovel, and I started getting better that night."

Any other day, I would have laughed. Today I ask, "How'd Mr. Buckley know what to look for?"

Your pa-paw shakes his head again, drops the milfoil in the water and watches it bob away. "He learned it growing up down in the holler. Lots of my friends' folks had come up from there after they flooded it. They'd tell stories about witches throwing curses and root-workers breaking them. Carry a lucky charm made from a buckeye or a stone with a hole in it, but thought you were crazy to walk around with two silver dollars in your pocket. That was tempting death, since when you died they put silver dollars on your eyes. They said you could heal bleeding by reading chapter sixteen of Ezekiel. And that you should never transplant a cedar tree from where it was growing. It was a different way of living down there, a whole different world."

"What about something like this? Somebody's soul getting trapped in the river?"

"No, I don't think so ... they talked about plenty of spooks, sure, but never anything like this. This river's so old, though. It's got so many secrets. Even someone like Mr. Buckley probably didn't know half of them."

"It has something to do with music," Tyler says. He rolls your tarnished ring between his fingers. "The catfish came right after I played, too."

"Rivercall! You're right!" I gasp as it hits me. "You played, then Holly sent the catfish to us. She can still hear the music somehow. She knows it's us somehow."

"But why can't she do more?" your pa-paw asks. "The first time I noticed the weeds doing that was days ago. I ain't budged from this spot since." He plucks another stalk of milfoil and tears it to bits. You musicians can't think without fiddling with something. Your brains are directly connected to your hands.

"Well … what if we're too far away?" I say. "Maybe we need to go to Swallow's Nest Bluff and play there."

Tyler's mouth goes slack. His eyes beg for mercy. "Jane, I—"

"It's where she drowned. Maybe she can't send us a clear message because she's too far away. We have to get as close to her as possible and pray she can tell us what's happening."

Tyler stares at his quivering reflection in the water. He wipes his eyes quickly. "I don't know if I can."

"You can. We have to."

"Jane, I—"

"What did that ring mean? Why did you give it to Holly?"

Tyler runs the tip of his pinky along the inside of the ring—silver, tarnished bruise-brown—but he stays mute. He moves it back and forth, letting sunlight shaped by the cut-out cross play across his fingertips.

"It was more than just some pretty little present, wasn't it?" I ask. "You wanted her to wear it and think of you, to remember you were always going to be there for her, always stand by her. Well, she remembers, Tyler. You think it was chance she used it to send her message? She remembers, and she needs you to remember."

Tyler nods. "You're right. You're right." All his goofiness is gone. The words fall heavy and certain like a lead weight in the palm.

Show me a sunbeam that can do that, Holly.

Your pa-paw gets the engine running while me and Tyler chop the houseboat loose from the milfoil. Tyler unwinds the docking ropes, then jumps back onboard as the boat eases out of its slip. The green and gray land passes in a shimmering heat-haze like a daydream. As the marina drifts away, Tyler takes the wheel from your pa-paw. Grown-ups can't find Swallow's Nest Bluff.

This river is so old. When the Nephilim walked the land and men were like grasshoppers at their feet, it was flashing as thin and quick as a minnow. The Mississippians came and built cities along its banks. They raised earthwork pyramids into the cool air and let the spring floods fertilize their fields with rich black silt. They carved images of eagle-beaked bird men and a monster called the underwater panther into clay. They believed animals able to move between the land, water, and sky—salamanders, turtles, ducks—and maybe catfish too?—acted as messengers of the gods, moving between our world and the spirit worlds above and below us.

The Mississippians lived and worshiped here for five hundred years, then disappeared. Nobody knows why. They vanished before Columbus came, leaving their warriors decaying within great burial mounds, surrounded by crumbling symbols of strength and wealth.

Hernando de Soto came through Muscle Shoals, exploring the New World. He forded the shoals heading into Tennessee and never came back down again. The Indians thought he was an immortal sun god. After he died of fever, his men were afraid of what the Indians might do if they discovered he'd just been a man. They weighted his body down with stones and tipped it over the side of a boat, letting the river swallow one more secret.

English and Irish settlers came and built a port on top of the Mississippians' great burial mounds, grown lush with wildflowers by then. During the Civil War, soldiers came. They're still here, too. From the highway, people have seen their ghosts marching, deaf and blind to the roaring cars.

It's all still here, Holly. People built the dam, tried to tame the river, let the lake cover up the Indian mounds, but it's all still down there. I can feel them all underneath us—curses of the Nephilim, the underwater panther, Hernando de Soto's bones clanking around in rusted-out armor, fevers disguised as frogs—one layer of mysteries on top of another on top of another. And you've sunk down, down to the lightless bottom and can't escape.

Thinking about it makes my stomach tighten; it makes breathing hard. But I won't be afraid, Holly. There is no fear in love, but perfect love casteth out fear.

Nine

Tyler scans the shoreline through his Aviators. Sitting on the deck, I try to pray for protection and guidance, but it's hopeless. I close my eyes, but all I feel is the river's long centuries, stretching back to the start of the world.

The bluff comes into view, a fist of striated limestone. I haven't been here since you died, Holly. Suddenly, I can't feel the lake anymore, only the hot, hard sadness swelling in my throat.

It was the height of summer. You were out of school, and Tyler just got his license. We went mud-riding across his cousin's land, bouncing up and down hills, spraying dirt. He let me drive some, and I fishtailed the truck just to feel the delicious whip-crack momentum bounce us against the doors.

We should have stayed out there, or just gone home. I'm sorry, Holly. But it felt like the start of everything. It was so much fun to go fast and be loud, we didn't want to stop. Tyler suggested we drive out to the bluff.

The water below us was pea-green and restless. We'd swing and jump, dangling in the air for a moment before gravity grabbed us by our stomachs and yanked us down. Flung hard to the water, the sting and cold-shock of it, making every nerve yowl at once, reminding us how alive we were.

Remember how excited you were about the Halogen concert? Since Tyler could drive now, you could go to shows in Huntsville, Birmingham, anywhere. Stretched out on the stone ledge, soaking in the sun, I decided to ask my parents if I could go to the concert with you.

While we talked, Tyler walked to the truck, then came back. "Hey, I got you something," he muttered, nervously pressing the ring box into your hands. When you opened it, your grin grew huge. "Oh, it's gorgeous!" you said, slipping the ring onto your finger. "Thank you, thank you!"

Tyler was grinning too. "Well, I didn't want you forgetting about me since we aren't seeing each other in class every day."

"Awww... I will never forget about you. Ever, ever." Wrapping your arms around his neck, you kissed him twice, quick little pecks. "Come on, let's jump together." Both of you holding the tire swing, you backed up and ran for the edge, planting a foot in the tire just as it sailed out over the lake. Holly, when you jumped, your ring winked in the sun. You hit the water with a massive double splash, then popped back up laughing. The swallows swooped down from their mud nests clumped across the bluff's stone face, crying and wheeling above your head.

Now, Tyler cuts the motor and we coast toward the bluff.

Your pa-paw drops the anchor from the aft deck. The anchor chain rattles down through the hawsehole for a long, long time, dropping all the way to the drowned forest. The swallows dive at the boat, scolding us, slicing the air a few feet above our heads. At the crucifixion, swallows screamed at the Roman soldiers, trying to warn them of the terrible crime they were committing, trying to stop them. That long, hot afternoon, they kept trying to warn us too, didn't they, Holly? I know that now.

But you and Tyler treaded water together, holding each other, giggling and kissing in the shade of overhanging pines. Swinging lazily on the tire swing, watching the two of you below, it struck me that my cousin had been about my age when she forgot about Swallow's Nest Bluff. We might not remember it either by next summer. I would have to bring Tim and his friends out here soon, before we lost the way.

But that day, with the cool breeze rolling off the lake, it was still our secret place. I called down, "Hey, Holly! Can you still do a backflip?"

You laughed. "Haven't done one in years."

"So? You still got it in you." I stuck a foot out and caught the earth again to stop the tire from swinging. "Come on, don't be a scaredy-cat. I'll do it with you."

Tyler joined in. "Come on, I want to see."

"Fine, okay. And just one, then we go home. The water's already getting too cold."

The bluff is steep. The only place to climb out of the water is a natural staircase of algae-slick stone. You climbed carefully, with Tyler close behind. The swallows cried and wheeled, but we ignored them. We stood inside the old rubber tire as Tyler dug his heels into the dirt and pulled it back. I remember the great branch overhead groaning, he pulled us so far. Then he let go. We whooped as emptiness rose up around us like a whale, swallowing us whole. We plunged down its throat, jumping high and fearless, scattering the shrieking birds. Our feet kicked the blue out of the sky.

We speared the water, and I lost sight of you. Momentum drove me down, down, until the black branches of the drowned forest licked at my heels. I started kicking back to the light, breaking the surface with a gasp that turned into a laugh. Tyler stood high on the bluff cheering. The water *was* getting cold, so I climbed out quick. By the time I reached the top of the bluff, though, Tyler had turned quiet and nervous. He was shielding his eyes from the glare of the setting sun.

"Holly? Holll-yyy!"

There was just the bull's-eye of ripples spreading out from where you'd vanished. Soon, they vanished too. The ancient water forgot you'd ever been there. That was when the knowing—even before I dared say it out loud—felt like gravity grabbing me by the stomach. The swallows never stopped screaming at us.

Your pa-paw steps onto the deck, startling me back to today. "Well, guys?"

"Guess we just play," Tyler says.

Nodding, your pa-paw swings his Dreadnought around. He picks out "Shave and a Haircut," then says, "I know. This one, Holly always liked," and teases a buttery-smooth melody from the strings.

Your pa-paw plays for the swallows and the bass boats slicing along the channel. An hour passes in drowsy stillness, in sweltering heat and the damp stink of river muck. Tyler climbs to the roof of the boat's cabin to see what he can see from there.

Dear Lord in Heaven, please help Holly. Please give us the strength to face whatever we must face.

Kneeling—the hard rubber deck hurts my knees—I try to pray. But every time I glance over the side, the milfoil has gotten a little thicker around us. I go back to the aft. Plant stalks wrap around the anchor chain and are tangled in the propellers.

"Stupid seaweed has us snagged again," I call out.

On the roof, Tyler nods. "Good. Means Holly is listening."

"But we need more than this. We need to know what to do."

"Give her time, Jane. We have to give her time."

I glance over the side again, trying to peer past the swaying weeds and murk. You dove down and got tangled in something on the bottom. The trees down there made it too dangerous for rescue divers, so we all just left you there. We had a funeral and said the prayers and buried a box full of letters and photos, but we left you down there, all alone inside the drowned forest. Is that why you can't rest, Holly?

"Come on, Holly," I whisper into the lapping, muttering water. "We're here. We're waiting. Tell us how to help you. Just tell us."

The last ember of sun burns down. It's dark but still sticky hot. Needing a break, your pa-paw calls Tyler down to take over playing. I duck into the cabin to get sweet tea for everybody. Tyler starts playing "The Drowned Forest," since that one already called you once. Bo must have talked to his parents by now. Tyler must be worried but doesn't let on.

Crunching an ice cube between my teeth—it tastes like pure, delicious cold—I sit with your pa-paw and listen to Tyler play. "You really think Holly'll know it's us?" I ask. "I mean, it's just music. It could be just a radio somebody left on."

Your pa-paw shakes his head. "Two people can't play a song the same way, even if they wanted to. Everybody puts their own style into it. I'd know Holly's style anywhere. She knows mine." Moths mob the deck light, creating a fluttering lace of shadows across his face. He adds, "My momma's been dead twenty years. Sometimes I hear songs in my dreams, and I'll know it's her playing them just from the way she played."

"Your mom played guitar?"

"Oh, goodness. She played fast and hot like a string of firecrackers."

I chuckle. In my mind's eye, I see the old woman from *American Gothic* rocking out, doing huge windmill strums.

"What's so funny? Everybody knew how to play a little down in the holler, or at least dance some. There wasn't any other way to knock the dirt off your boots. And Momma, she played like you thought the house was burning…down." He turns.

A soft splashing comes from the stern. We all turn, but the deck lights blind us, turning the darkness beyond them construction-paper black. Something rattles up the anchor chain. It's climbing out of the water and over the railing.

"Pa-paw?"

Dashing, crowding the gangway, we yell over one another. "Holly, we're here!" "It's okay!" "Holly, Holly!"

Crawling into the light, you're thin, thinner than I could imagine. Your skin is dusky red like a newborn's. It's the color of dried blood. "Pa-paw? Help."

Dropping to his knees, he holds you. "I'm here, Little Bit."

"Pa-paw, I'm cold." Arms hug his neck. You cling to him like ivy.

Your skin is … clay. It's damp red Alabama clay. It splits when you move, and pale spikes of milfoil grow between the cracks.

But your pa-paw is crying and doesn't notice. He sobs, "It's okay, Holly. We're here. Tyler, get a towel or something."

Tyler doesn't move. His mouth opens, but he can't speak. Where your fingers clutch your pa-paw's shoulder, gnarled bark breaks through his skin. The cloth of his shirt rots and blackens with blood.

"Mr. Alton, you need to get—"

"A towel, Tyler! Get a towel!" As he twists around, your fingers dig deeper. Hickory twigs tremble up from his back, the leaves already yellow and orange.

"Mr. Alton, get back! Get away!"

He fights to break free, dead leaves rattling. More branches sprout along the curve of his collar bone. His eyes bulge and veins in his neck turn purple as he suffocates, but then the creature cries, "Pa-paw!" and he stops trying to get away. Still struggling to breathe, he reaches for the thing that has your voice.

"Pa-paw, I don't know where we are."

He holds the creature until roots split his elbows and wrists and between his fingers, swallowing his arms in squirming white clumps. His face and chest are mostly gone, but the creature still whimpers and hugs the stunted hickory tree that's sinking its taproot into the boat deck. Nut husks break open and spill their dry brown fruit.

We run away. Moving is hard. It's like running through mud. It's like in my nightmares. Duck through the hatch, down into the cabin. I trip and fall, twisting my wrist. It doesn't hurt even though I know it should.

"Tyler?"

He slams the hatch and locks it.

"Tyler, what is that thing?"

"I don't know."

"Why did it kill Mr. Alton?"

"I don't know!"

"Tyler?" the monster croaks from outside. "Tyler, let me in."

It starts scratching at the hatch. Black-eyed Susans and wedding-white hydrangeas sprout through the varnish. I yank the curtains shut so it can't see us. "We have to go. Get to shore, then we can run."

"The anchor is down, Jane. The milfoil has tangled the propeller. We're stuck."

I turn the key anyway, listening to the engine groaning *rarr…rarr…rarr…* as it struggles to turn the propeller. We're trapped. The thing lured us here, trapped us, and then killed Mr. Alton.

The wooden hatch rots away, and a breeze carries the

pungent smell of river muck into the cabin. The mud-thing, coughed up from the drowned forest, moans as it pushes through. "Jane?"

I crumple to the floor, crushing myself between the captain's chair and the steering console. It finds me, though, and the crooked gash of a mouth opens into a smile. It reaches for me. I scream, and it pulls back.

"Jane? Wh—what's the matter?" It's your voice. Wet and weak, but it's your voice.

"Holly?"

"Jane." Sunny yellow dandelions blink open. "I got lost. We—we were diving off the bluff, but then I got lost somehow. I've been wandering around for . . . Pa-paw was here, but then he . . ." You search the cabin, confused, then look back at me. The horrible smile widens, displacing your jaw. "I knew you'd come. Just like the time with the church flower gardens, remember? Remember?"

This monster is you, Holly. Dead and come back to life—back to some ramshackle version of life—clumps of mud and weeds matted together—but it's you. I shut my eyes and whimper. Fingers clutch my shirt, scratch my skin. The reek of your sludgy skin chokes me. "Stop, Jane. Please, I can't find my way—"

Tyler puts his full force into the kick, knocking you off me, knocking off half your face. He grabs me by the arm, yanks me up, screaming, "The aft hatch. C'mon!"

The floor buckles underneath us. The hull has already rotted where you were crouched. Cold water swirls in around our ankles.

"No, don't go! Jane!"

"Holly…I'm…" But there aren't any words. I turn and run. The boat is listing to one side, but we get past the sleeping berths and through the aft hatch, jumping for the shiny black water.

Ten

The river swallows me. It slurps me down a throat of bubbles and swirling noise, down, down into water as silent and dark as a womb.

I kick at the blackness, kicking back up toward the air and Tyler's wail. "—aaaane! Jaaaane!"

"Over here!" I wave until he sees me.

"You okay?"

I don't know how to answer that. "Where's Holly?"

"Still onboard, I think. You hurt? Can you swim?"

I'm not hurt, so we start to swim. The houseboat—and you—squat between us and the bluff, so we make for the north shore. I focus on the downtown lights crowding along the embankment. Cars speed across the dam. From a concert in the Veterans Park amphitheater, brassy notes carry out across the lake. Behind us, the houseboat slips lower and lower, then vanishes with a great sploosh and waves that ripple out beneath me. For a few seconds, cabin lights shimmer under the water. I turn and watch it sinking down. Then the generator shorts and the hull goes dark.

Treading water, I look for you, but nothing moves.

"Jane! Come on!"

I start swimming again, muscles burning. Where are you? Under the water? Trapped in the houseboat or chasing after us? Can the thing you've become swim? Do you have to come up for air? I keep going, waiting for you to grab my ankle and pull me down. As we cross above the drowned forest, I can feel it below us, barren branches reaching up like hands, waiting to embrace me.

But it doesn't happen. We make it to the park, down from the shining amphitheater. Years of lapping waves have licked a hollow below the walking trail. Tyler tries climbing up but doesn't have the strength. He slumps back to the soft red clay, catching his breath, holding on to an exposed root. "Okay. Okay. We're okay," he pants.

I've lost my flip-flops. I rub the scratches you left on my arm and hand. They're swollen and angry red, and there's a weird sort of pressure from under my skin, like it wants to pucker open.

"My truck's still at the marina. We have to—"

"Tyler? J-Jane?"

We whip around, but there's nobody—no body. Just your thin voice in the dark.

"Where ... are?" A crack widens in the clay bank. No lips, no teeth, but a slug-like tongue moves inside.

"Tyler ... need help."

I can't take this. Please, please don't do this, Holly.

The clay shifts. Something like a shoulder pushes upward. An eye opens.

"Jane?"

Tyler grabs the waistband of my shorts, heaving me up onto the grass, then scrambles after me. We run past the dark picnic shelter. Tyler checks his cell phone, but it's wet and ruined. He cusses and smashes it to the gravel path.

Reaching the road, he sticks close to the low wall, stopping to think. "Stratofortress! They live close by. Come on."

Crusting mud cakes my legs and hands. Tyler's sneakers squelch with water. The sidewalk is fever-hot under my bare feet, but I can still feel the cold of the drowned forest below.

No, the cold isn't under me anymore. It's inside. It's termite-tunneling through skin and muscle. Delicate flowers emerge from the scratches on my arm, my hand—sticky, hairy stalks and tight buds already unfolding. "Ty-Tyler?"

He looks over. And because he still has shoes, he heaves me onto his back and starts jogging. "Hang on, just ... hang on ... please."

I wrap my arms around his neck and cling to him. When you scratched me, you left some essence of the drowned forest under my skin. I can feel roots probing, teasing skin away from muscle, soul from bone. They're reaching for my heart, but it doesn't hurt. Their coolness feels nice on such a hot, humid night.

Staring up past the streetlamps, I can't see the stars anymore, Holly. Can't you remember our nights down here? Burning to rush around and be loud and be alive, and who cared that the stars were all gone? I miss you so much. I don't want to grow up without you. I can't, Holly. The drowned forest is in my head now. Its voice is a lullaby, hypnotic like gentle waves lapping the shore. It promises death will be easy, like relaxing a clenched fist. Dying will be less painful than living.

No, no, I don't care. I want to live. I press myself against Tyler's back, and I want to live. That's all I know—one greedy breath after another.

There's the shabby house, overflowing ashtrays still on the porch. The gate is padlocked. Tyler tips me over the fence like a sack of potatoes. He lands hard in the dirt beside me. "Come on, come on." He grabs my hand, pulling me up. Banging on the front door, calling out. Finally LeighAnn appears.

"Hey. What's ... holy hell, what's going on?"

Tyler pushes past her without answering, dragging me along too.

Max is wearing shorts and no shirt. "She's got ... are those flowers?"

"We need to pull them out." Tyler leads me to the living room couch. Somebody kicks the drum kit. The thump bounces off carpeted walls.

Max turns on a lamp and runs careful fingers across the leaves and petals. "How ... ? How is that even happening?"

Tyler shakes his head. "Later. First, we just get them out."

Max holds my arm while Tyler plucks one of the flowers. Root torn from muscle—I scream, body bowing up.

"We should get her to a hospital, man. If we—"

"No." I shake my head. The roots have reached past my elbow. They're part of me. I feel the blossoms open with a sugary sort of fizzing. "They'll kill me before we get there. Pull them out. Please, please."

Tyler pulls one. I grit my teeth against the pain but can't keep from screaming again. LeighAnn cradles my head, wiping sweat away with the hem of her T-shirt. She murmurs, "Doing good. Almost through. Doing good."

I'm too tired to scream anymore, so I just whimper. Tyler plucks the last one. "Jane? That was it, Jane. You okay?"

My skin looks scraped raw. Blood trickles down, turning gummy in the creases of my palm.

"Okay, what … what the hell?" LeighAnn asks.

Tyler's face is fish-belly white and slick with sweat. "Something attacked us out on the lake. It pretended to be Holly and lured us out there, then—"

"No." I sit up. "That was Holly. I mean, her body was mud and weeds, but I talked to her. It's Holly's soul inside."

"No. Holly would never kill her pa-paw."

"Whoa. Somebody was killed?" LeighAnn asks.

"She didn't do it on purpose, Tyler. I don't think she knows she's dead."

"Um, how about we figure all this out on the way to the ER?" Max asks.

"No." I half sit up. "I can't go to the hospital."

"There were plants growing through your skin!" He pushes his glasses up, leaving a red smear on the lens.

"They're gone. I can feel it." Standing makes my head

spin, but I force myself not to puke. "I just need to wash the cuts real good. You have any antibiotic ointment?"

I follow Max down the hall to the bathroom. The hallway wall is covered in dozens of concert flyers, some of them wrinkled from rain. In the green-tiled bathroom, Max gets ointment and gauze from under the sink, then steps out. I pull my phone out of my pocket. It won't turn on anymore. My dad once dropped his phone in a puddle, then stuck it in a bowl of rice to draw out the moisture. But I went swimming with my phone, so I doubt that would work. The only other thing in my pocket is the twenty-dollar bill. I unfold it carefully and lay it on the counter to dry.

Next, I peel off my shirt and wash my arm under the tub faucet. The water turns pink as I scrub away blood and mud. The pain makes my hands shake. Muscles tighten into ropes. My face twists shut like the top of a plastic bag.

You killed your pa-paw, Holly. We were coming to save you, and you killed him, and you don't even know what you've done or what you've become. What happened to you down in the drowned forest?

I flex my fingers. My arm still burns, deep in the muscle, when I do. I want to go to the ER. They could zap my arm with about a million x-rays to make sure every last root tip was dead. I want to go home. Even if Mom and Dad are furious, I'd just hug them tight. Even if they sent me to Dr. Haq or grounded me for a year or gave me a lobotomy, I wouldn't care.

I want to give up, Holly.

I want to run back home and never talk about this night. Resting my forehead on the tub's cool lip, I beg God to let this cup pass from me. But God has forsaken us, left us both blowing in the wind.

And you had to talk about the church flower gardens.

I open the cabinet under the sink and find some Windex. Unscrewing the spray top, I pour it across my arm. The ammonia and detergents seep down into the tiny cuts, killing off any root tips still buried under my skin. It burns like the edge of a hot pan. I bite down on a hand towel and empty the bottle.

I won't forsake you, Holly, no matter what.

I smear ointment on my arm and bandage it. I fix my ponytail in the mirror and shove my fear down into a tight knot inside my chest. I can still feel it, but I can also walk and talk and force a smile. For once, I'm glad I can't cry.

Tyler and the others are still in the living room.

"…I don't know," Max says. "A catfish and ring, some ghost made from mud. It's just pretty hard to believe."

"Well, you pulled flowers out of my skin," I say from the archway. "You saw that yourself, right? You believe your own eyes, right?"

Tyler looks over his shoulder. "Hey. You okay?"

I step past him, continuing to talk to Max and LeighAnn. "I know it's nuts. I've spent the last day trying to figure out how everything I'm seeing must not be what's actually happening. I'd be a lot happier if somebody could convince me I'm crazy. But Tyler sees the same things I do. And now you guys have seen it. What's happening is what's happening, and what I'm seeing is what I'm seeing. Here." I offer my wounded, scabbing arm to them. "Feel the cuts if you want, but really, what's happening is what's happening."

Neither of them take me up on my offer. Max says, "Okay, what's happening is what's happening, but, I mean, what *is* happening?"

I shake my head. "Don't know yet. But I need a big favor. I need somewhere to stay until we figure that out, and figure out how to help Holly."

"Jane..." Tyler shakes his head. "Are you sure that's really Holly?"

"Yes. She talked about stuff only she'd know about. She's scared and confused, but that's Holly."

Tyler doesn't argue. I look at the others again. "My parents won't believe any of this. They haven't seen it, so they can't believe it. And if I keep talking about it, they'll probably have me committed or something. My friends from church won't believe it, our pastor, he... I just need to stay somewhere until we figure out what to do. I... I can't really pay right now—"

"Nah, don't worry about that. You know how many freeloaders have crashed here?" Max slaps the worn couch cushion. "You'll be sleeping in the buttprints of giants."

"Except none of them had some sort of river ghost after them," LeighAnn says. "What if it comes here and attacks us?"

"Lee-Lee, we can't just kick her out."

LeighAnn snorts. "Some people, a few nights on the street might be good for them." She walks off without another word.

Max agrees to drive Tyler back over to the marina to get his truck. First, he finds me a sleeping bag and pillow. I wish he'd offer me some dry clothes to sleep in, but he doesn't. And I don't want to ask these people for any more than I have to.

I wish Tyler could stay, but he has his own parents to worry about. Hopefully he can keep them from freaking. Hugging me tight, he says, "We'll figure something out, okay? It's going be okay."

I smile and answer, "I hope so," even though I know he's wrong. Maybe we'll figure out how to save you, Holly, but I know in my soul that it's not going to be okay. It's going to be hard and dangerous, and I don't think anything will ever really be okay again.

Tyler and Max head off. LeighAnn stomps around the kitchen. I lie on the sagging couch and pretend to be asleep. The house is sweltering. There's no air conditioning, just some open windows letting in a weak breeze and cricket song.

Eleven

The door bursts open, and where am I? I yell, groping through unfamiliar shadows.

The light comes on, making me wince. "Jane? Hey." Ultimate Steve stands under the hard glare.

"Hey." I'm at Stratofortress's house, I remember now. I remember everything.

Steve is wearing the same clothes he had on yesterday morning. Sipping an energy drink, he says, "So…what? You crashing here?"

I nod. "Holly's a ghost. Her soul's trapped in the river, and I have to stay here until we can free her."

"Wow, that sucks. It won't keep you up if I play Xbox, will it?" He's already down on the floor in front of the TV. I shut my eyes, but machine-gun fire from the game washes over me, keeps making me flinch. I open one eye.

"Didn't you just drive to South Carolina and back?"

"Yeah." His face flickers in blue light, then in the bright orange of a tossed grenade.

"So aren't you going to get some sleep?"

"Nah, had, like, twelve of these things." He takes another gulp of his energy drink.

I pull the lip of the sleeping bag over my head. My skin is damp and itchy from my wet clothes. Plus I don't have my Tenex. I'll never get back to sleep.

Lying hidden, I drift back to the time the youth group planted flowers in the church flower beds. Two springs ago? We were supposed to do it on a Wednesday evening, but bad weather pushed it to Saturday. Mom and me were both scrambling to make sure enough people came, and I couldn't figure out why you were so mad.

"You were gonna come over here on Saturday." Your anger crackled over the phone.

"Well, stuff got turned around because of the rain. Sorry."

"We were gonna make monkey bread."

"We'll make it some other time."

"I wanted to do it Saturday. Please, we haven't hung out in forever."

"Well, we've got five pallets of impatiens that need to be planted. Why can't you come and help?"

"I can't deal with Jonathan. All the youth group guys are just…"

"What?"

"Nothing."

"They're just what?" I snapped, getting mad.

"They're goof-offs, Jane. They'll work for, like, fifteen

minutes, then start goofing off and make you do the rest." Several seconds of staticky silence passed, then you muttered, "Why do you have to be in charge of every single youth group project, anyway? You're such a goody-goody."

"I am not." My lame response just made me madder at you. "I have to go. Have fun sitting in your house judging everybody."

"Yeah, whatever." You hung up, the buzz of the dead line stinging like a wasp. You were angry because I couldn't bake monkey bread with you. Angry because under the surface, beneath all your sweetness, there was always something desperate, something half-convinced that everybody had already abandoned you.

That's what came out of the water last night … that frightened, always-hungry shadow of yourself. That can't be all that's left of you, Holly. It just can't.

That morning, we filled the flowerbeds with fresh potting soil before planting. Then we gently teased each impatiens's root ball loose before setting it into the rain-dampened ground. I love the smell of humus—that old vegetable matter decayed into rich, dark dirt. Planting things, sinking my hands into the cool earth, may be the most calming feeling in the world, the most *right* feeling in the world.

But that day, I was mad because you were acting like a jerk. I got even madder when the boys started goofing off fifteen minutes in, chasing each other around the community hall.

But I prayed for you, Holly, right there on the sidewalk, clasped hands black with dirt. And when I prayed, I stopped feeling mad, and when I stopped feeling mad, I remembered it was the anniversary of your parents' death.

"Oh no." I stood up. "Jonathan! Come here! I need you guys to plant the rest of this row. And that row over there."

"Okay," he chuckled. "But Dylan took my—"

"I don't care! I have to do something, and all these have to get in the ground today."

"Okay, okay. But how do we—"

"Figure it out." Stuffing my straw hat on his head, I left. Just turned my back and walked away. That felt good, Holly, I have to admit.

I jogged the two miles to your house. By the time I knocked on the door, I was panting hard. But when you opened it, I managed enough breath to snap, "Why didn't you tell me what today was?"

"I don't—did your mom drop you off or something?"

"I was at church and ran."

"You ran?"

"Yes, of course," I said, stepping into the delicious air conditioning of your living room. "Where's your pa-paw?"

"At the studio," you grumbled. "He always finds something to work on this time of year. He'll probably put in a hundred hours this week."

I sighed and asked again, "Why didn't you just tell me?"

"Because it's stupid."

"No, it's not." I pulled you into a hug. "*You're* stupid for not telling me. But this is not stupid."

Burying your face in my neck, you began to sob. "Part of me just can't ever remember that they're dead. Sometimes

I wake up in the middle of the night and think they're in the next room. And then I remember, and it's almost like losing them all over."

"I'm so sorry."

"I miss Mom and Dad. I miss Me-maw."

"I know, I know. But I'm always here for you, Holly. All you ever have to do is ask. Okay?"

You sniffled and nodded, then said, "Can't believe you ran all the way here."

"Yeah. Oh, I also yelled at Jonathan."

"Really? Awesome."

Twelve

The shower turns on. Is it morning already? I lie in my sleeping bag thinking about you, thinking about my promise. Max and Steve talk in the kitchen. I smell black coffee and pick out my name in their conversation. Tyler's name too.

"See you tonight, Lee-Lee," Max says.

"Bye, guys. Be careful."

They walk out. A motor starts and pulls away. Then LeighAnn nudges me. "Hey. Hey, wake up."

Pulling down the lip of the sleeping bag, I squint at her. She's wearing a white blouse and maroon skirt. The airplane tattoo on her forearm shows through the thin material of her blouse, but she pulls on a maroon suit jacket that covers it completely. She looks normal now, except for a pair of bangles on her wrist made from old guitar strings.

Flipping her hair out of her collar, LeighAnn asks, "You okay? No...?" She mimes a flower blooming.

"Yeah, I'm okay." Kicking out of the sleeping bag, I scratch at my bandages.

"I got some clothes for you. If you want to wash what you've got on."

"Thanks." The denim shorts and well-worn tee smell like cigarettes, but at least they're dry. The old sneakers are at least a size too big. "How come you're dressed like that?"

"Going to work."

"Oh. I thought you were in a band."

She snorts. "Yeah, well, rock 'n' roll's just the money gig. My passion is being a bank teller. Want some coffee?"

"No thanks."

"Well, it's there if you change your mind. Not much else food-wise. Some sandwich stuff, I think. Ravioli and some canned stuff in the laundry room."

For a table, Stratofortress has a giant cable spool in the middle of the dining room, *Florence Utilities* stenciled across the top. Dishes lie stacked in the kitchen sink, a fly buzzing round them. I really don't want to eat anything from here, but I make myself say, "Thanks. And thanks for letting me stay here."

"Mmhmm." Her eyes widen suddenly and she says, "Hey, we're going to go see a band later tonight. Want to come with us?"

"Oh, no. Thanks, but I—"

"Band called the Herpes Sponges. Sure you don't want to come?"

"Uh, yeah." That's what I called LeighAnn yesterday. My face burns from the memory. My throat tightens. But she says it calmly, a rushed, half-remembered thing. Maybe it's a coincidence. Maybe God is just reminding—

"Kinda ticks me off, actually. I was going to start a band called the Herpes Sponges. Or, you know, name my first child Herpes Sponge. Herpes Sponge Cassell. It's more of a girl's name, but it could work for a boy, don't you think?"

I stare hard at the floor.

"Well? What do you think?"

"I . . . I don't know."

Is she going to kick me out? Holly, where do I go now?

"You think I'm trashy, fine. I'll still take care of your runaway butt. But don't *ever* treat me like I'm stupid."

I nod, trying to cough up some chalk-dry apology. Then LeighAnn's expression suddenly brightens again. "And if you can walk the dogs sometime today, that'd be a major help. Leashes are above the dryer. See you." She turns and walks off. The front door opens and bangs shut.

My hands tremble with relief. Or guilt. Or both. LeighAnn could have kicked me out—she had a right to—but some spark of grace kept her from dumping me out on the street. Holly, I have to remember that. I hug the clothes LeighAnn loaned me. No matter what else I think about her, about these people, I have to remember that.

Outside, dawn hangs over the backyards like blue chiffon. The air remains night-cool and damp, but it'll heat up soon. I go change into the clothes LeighAnn lent me. It feels good pulling on clean things. Right away, I'm sorry for acting stupid and stubborn last night and not asking to borrow something.

I unwrap the bandages from my arm. Scabs and bruises mark where you scratched me, Holly. One sickly pale flower has grown under the bandage, curled flat against my skin. I prod at the silk thread of a stem. Part of my soul stretches into the flower. I can sense the delicious cool against the leaves. I taste the drop of musky sweetness hidden at the center of squashed petals. I pinch the flower's base and yank. The blood on the roots is bright red. Smearing on more antibiotic ointment, re-wrapping my arm, I toss the little flower in the trash.

I want to go home. My parents have probably been up all night worrying about me, praying, waiting for me to call. I wish I could at least text them so they'd know I'm okay. Stratofortress has a landline phone hanging on the kitchen wall. I could call Mom and Dad, just tell them I love them. But the police might trace the call. They'd come get me, and Mom and Dad wouldn't let me out of their sight afterward.

I can't go home. It doesn't matter how lonely I feel. It doesn't matter how much it hurts Mom and Dad. I can't go home until I know you're safe. I force the idea away, deciding to distract myself by nosing around Stratofortress's house.

The flyers lining the hallway are from lots of different bands and venues—Calamity Jane in Birmingham, the Suicide Kings and Tom Waits in Nashville, a ton of shows at the UNA student center. There's only a few flyers from Stratofortress's own gigs. They're all for local shows at the Brick or the Bandito Burrito. Stratofortress is usually an opening act, and on one flyer, they're listed as Stradivarius.

I look around the rest of the house. In LeighAnn and Max's bedroom, a thick layer of clothes and sound equipment covers the floor. A marijuana pipe sits on the dresser, ribbons of purple running through its clear glass body. Ultimate Steve doesn't have a bed, just a mattress on the floor. A Jolly Roger hangs across the window for a curtain. A hole in the ceiling exposes the roof joists like two-by-four ribs, and a pot on the floor catches dripping water.

I want to go home, Holly.

No, no, it doesn't matter. I have to push the idea out of my head.

Back in the kitchen, I pour myself some coffee. The bitter black crud scalds my tongue, but at least it'll keep me awake. I check out the fridge. Almost no food, but there is half a case of beer.

Seriously, LeighAnn? You seriously want to be this particular rock 'n' roll cliché? I'm a home-schooled Jesus dork, and even I know how lame this is.

I shut the refrigerator door. They're letting me stay here. Remember that, remember that.

I heat up some ravioli for breakfast. Rinsing my bowl, I balance it on the stack of dishes already in the sink and start to walk away. But I can help out some while I'm here. Filling the sink with hot water, I wash the dishes. I need a butter knife to scrape away the crusty food and dead mosquito-eaters.

Tyler should be up by now. I wonder if Bo told his parents everything. I pace and worry, but I'll just have to wait until Tyler gets in touch with me. A sliding glass door leads from the kitchen to the back patio. I step out to see what kind of dogs LeighAnn has.

She has happy dogs! They scramble out of their doghouse

and come greet me, nails clicking on the bare concrete patio. I let them sniff my hand and check their tags to see their names. Hobbit has some golden retriever in him. Cookie is black and white and looks like a furry pig. I find the leashes, and we head up the street of dingy houses.

We pass two blocks from church, but I can't go there. Somebody would see me and tell. But I can't wait anymore, either. As soon as we return to Stratofortress's house, I call Tyler.

He answers halfway through the second ring. "Hello?"

"Hey, it's me. Is everything okay?"

"Yeah, pretty much. What about you?"

"Pretty much. So, did Bo tell your parents anything?"

"Yeah."

"Well? What happened?"

Tyler's voice drops to a whisper. "I'm not in trouble, but I can't really talk about it on the phone."

"Then come over here so we can talk."

"I can't right now. I have to get to school. And my folks are still suspicious."

"Well, make up some excuse or something. We have to figure out what to do, Tyler."

"I'll come over later today."

"Whatever." I slam the phone back onto the hook. Scowling and too anxious to sit still, I decide to clean some more. I wash my dirty clothes from last night, sweep the floors, and empty the ashtrays on the porch. It burns off excess energy, which makes me feel in control, and I start thinking about stuff I can do without Tyler, like maybe checking the library for any stories about ghosts around Wilson Lake. By lunch-time, I have a choice between tackling the bathroom or going to the library.

Grabbing my twenty-dollar bill, I step outside and start walking.

Twenty dollars, Holly. That's all I've got. At the Shop-Rite, I walk in and buy the number one thing: a toothbrush. With that stuffed in my front pocket, I head to the library. The sun's rays scrape at the back of my neck. I pick at my chapped bottom lip until I taste blood. One change of borrowed clothes. No phone. Seventeen dollars and twenty-one cents. How long can I live on this? A couple days? A week?

But hey, I'm at least one toothbrush better off than I was last night, right?

The public library doesn't have anything about local ghosts except that kids' book *13 Alabama Ghosts and Jeffery*. Remember scaring ourselves silly reading that, Holly?

With nothing much else to do, I walk to the University of North Alabama campus and check out their library. Students are typing at the computers and sifting through shelves of old journals. They camp out in their study carrels with notebooks, drinks, and fast-food bags. Half of them have their shoes kicked off.

I can't find anything useful in the computer database, so I ask at the reference desk. It takes the librarian twenty minutes of scrounging in the back, but he returns with two bulging manila envelopes.

From 1986 to 1989, a professor named Harry Frazier did interviews about magic and witchcraft with country people all around the Tennessee Valley. The envelopes are labeled *2 (of 6)* and *3 (of 6)*, and one has *Folklore Book KEEP!!!* scrawled across it in blue ink. Maybe Frazier was planning on writing a history of the valley or something. Inside, there's one audio cassette marked *Witherspoon #3* and a bunch of paper transcripts.

HF: Tell me about hot foot powder.

DW: Hot foot powder is what you sprinkle into a footprint if you don't want somebody coming around anymore. See, as they're leaving, you sprinkle their footprint in the dirt with the powder and mix it up real good, and then they'll never come back. It turns people restless if they try, can't get settled or feel comfortable.

HF: How is it made?

DW: A root-worker will get some river mud they dry out and grind up fine. The river, that's where the power comes from. Other ingredients get the person bothered real bad, like poison sumac or hot pepper.

HF: Do you know of anybody using hot foot powder?

DW: Sure, more than I could name. It's real common if, like, a girl has a boy who keeps hanging around and won't leave her alone. She'll get some hot foot powder to get rid of him. And I know two women who used it to drive off their husbands. One because he beat her real bad. The other, she just had another man.

The transcripts were typed on a typewriter, and sometimes there's just the pink carbon copy. Hunching over until my shoulders ache, ignoring my growling hunger, I read about weather signs, recipes for medicines and charms, and how to know if a witch has cursed your cow. Then one interview turns toward bogeymen and ghosts.

HF: Have you heard of Tommy Mud-and-Sticks?

MP: Yes sir, he was a spirit trapped in the river. Everybody down in the holler knew about Tommy Mud-and-Sticks, knew to run if they heard him crying.

HF: So he's a ghost? A dead spirit?

MP: Yes sir, he was drowned by his brother.

HF: Can you tell me the story?

MP: As best as I know, Tommy was married to a girl named Sharon, but she had an eye for his brother too. So one day, Tommy and his brother went hunting, and the brother knocked Tommy in the head and drowned him in the river. He told everybody it was an accident, and everybody believed him at first. But then Tommy came back. He cried out how his brother attacked him and that he had to find his wife. As soon as they got wind of that, Tommy's brother and Sharon ran off. Nobody knows where. But Tommy still came out of the river some nights, crying for Sharon. Especially if any blonde woman went down to the riverbank. Tommy might think she's his Sharon and drag her into the river with him. He didn't understand it'd been years since his Sharon ran off.

HF: How did he get the name "Mud-and-Sticks"?

MP: Well, sir, he was dead and rotting on the river bottom. I'm sorry, I don't know how to put it any nicer than that. So he made a new body out of mud, twigs, weeds all tangled together, stuff like that. Like his spirit, inside a body made of clay. There might have been a tooth in there that was still his, maybe some bones or some hair, maybe not even that.

As I read, my heart starts thumping. He dragged them into the river? Or maybe he made them rot away, and when they couldn't find a body, people figured he'd dragged them off. Or maybe the details just got confused in the retelling. But the rest is too close to be an accident.

That's all there is, though. Dr. Frazier doesn't ask how to get rid of Tommy Mud-and-Sticks or how to protect yourself from him. Instead he starts asking about a creature named Rawhead. It doesn't seem like he takes any of it seriously, thinking they're just spooky stories. I flip back to the beginning of the interview, where Dr. Frazier wrote a few paragraphs about the person he was talking to.

Mattie Peake's family had a small farm in Lauderdale County, Alabama. This farm lay within the impoundment of Wilson Dam. The subject was eight years old in 1924, when work on the dam was completed and the area was flooded. Her family was removed to a farm in Belle Mina, in Morgan County, Alabama, an action for which the subject still harbors resentment to this day. The Belle Mina community saw the resettlement of multiple families from the Wilson Dam impoundment, which led to the preservation of old superstitions and beliefs. For a time, Belle Mina was known as the place to go for root-worker "medicines" or hexes. The subject states she learned root-work chiefly from her grandfather, who lived with the family and often enlisted her help gathering plants and mixing medicines.

The subject completed the eighth grade and can read and write competently. After getting married, she moved to Decatur, Alabama, where her husband supervised a warehouse in the Decatur Harbor until his retirement two years ago. The couple have four adult children. The subject is well-regarded in the community, often called "Auntie Peake." She still mixes up medicines in her kitchen, prays over people who come to her for help, and claims to know if somebody is under a witch's hex or not. She does not charge for these services, as is the nearly universal custom among root-workers interviewed.

I skim through the rest of the transcripts, but neither Auntie Peake nor Tommy Mud-and-Sticks is mentioned again. I go back up to the reference desk. "Excuse me, hey.

These envelopes are marked two and three of six. Don't you have the others?"

The librarian shakes his head. "That's all I could find, sorry. Dr. Frazier died maybe ten years back, and they threw out most of the stuff in his office. I really don't know why these two were catalogued at all."

We're so close to an answer, my stomach feels tight and the back of my neck prickles. I beg him to look again. He does, but comes back five minutes later shaking his head some more. I want to throw the transcripts at him, Holly.

At least the librarian finds an old cassette player so I can listen to the Witherspoon tape. It hardly matters, though—the tape has deteriorated. No matter how much I fiddle with the buttons and spindles, the voices are half lost in a hiss of static.

"…a powerful root-worker. He mostly worked Godly magic, but if somebody crossed him or his, he knew a hex…" "…dug into the Indian mound and found it. Looked like a regular piece of quartz, but with colors inside like an oil slick. But if he looked through it and…" "…nesting in your roof will protect your house from lightning, but if the swallows ever abandon their nests, it means somebody in the house is going to…" "…kept like a pet. Except when I was little, sometimes I'd come over, and it'd be walking on its hind legs or sitting in the rocker like a person. I was too young to know that wasn't natural…"

The rest is murmuring voices, like people talking in their sleep. I strain to listen, but it's hopeless. Muscles in my back and arms tighten down with frustration. I want to scream. It takes physical effort to keep from smashing my fist against the tape player. Instead, I take everything back to the reference desk and thank the librarian for his help. As I leave, I feel lost and mad. I want to kick something. I want to curl up on the sidewalk and sob and give up.

Back at Stratofortress's house, I grab the mail out of the beat-up mailbox. Turns out Max's full name is Osgood Maxwell. Weird. I play with LeighAnn's dogs, barefoot in the backyard, spiny grass poking my soles. When I hear the rumble of Tyler's truck out front, I rush around and let him through the front gate. "So? What did Bo tell your parents?"

"Everything. All about the ring, you running away."

"Son of a biscuit!" Leading him back around to the backyard, I ask, "Well? Did they freak?"

"Yeah. They got scared when I didn't answer my phone last night, but I told them I was jamming with Ultimate and didn't hear it."

"They bought that?"

"Sure." He shrugs. "Same thing happened last week."

"So what about the ring and all that?"

"I, uh . . . I sort of put it all on you. Said I never really thought it was from Holly, but you were freaking out, and I was just sort of humoring you."

"Great. Thanks."

"It was the only thing I could think of. Sorry."

I throw a stick for the dogs. Hobbit ignores it, lying down in a hole he's dug. Cookie runs after the stick but won't bring it back. He gnaws off the bark, leaving a jagged pale tip that looks like bone. Your bones are still in the drowned forest, mixed with the black mud. Your pa-paw's bones are down there too, I guess, if you left him any bones after you were done with him. I remember how he stopped fighting when you embraced him, just quit, and my stomach suddenly hurts. I ask, "So what about Mr. Alton?"

"There's nothing in the newspaper. The houseboat sunk. Nobody even realizes he's missing yet."

"So what do we do?"

Tyler shrugs again. "What can we do? You've got to stay out of sight, so we can't go to the police. And even if we did, they wouldn't believe us. Or worse, they'll decide we'd murdered him."

"You're horrible." I grab the stick from Cookie and throw it again.

"Jane ..."

"He was Holly's grandpa, Tyler. And you just want to do nothing? He was a human being." But Tyler's right; there's nothing we *can* do. Holly, we've messed everything up so bad and can't fix it. It's just easier to dump on Tyler than admit this.

He says, "You want to do right by Mr. Alton? Then we finish what he started. We find a way to put Holly's soul to rest."

I nod. "Maybe you're right."

"So ... any ideas on how to do that?"

"Not any good ones, but I did go to the library today." I tell him about Tommy Mud-and-Sticks and Auntie Peake. He gets excited, just like I did. Then I have to give him the bad news. "She was an old woman when she did that interview back in the eighties. She might be dead by now, and even if she isn't, we don't have a phone number or anything. All we know is she lived in Decatur."

"Well, it's still more than we had yesterday. Maybe we can get in touch with her. Maybe she can tell us what's going on."

I nod just as we hear the front gate swinging open again. It's Max and Steve. We go inside through the sliding glass door and meet them in the kitchen. They're both sweaty and flushed, wearing Florence Utilities work shirts. Steve carries a grocery sack. "How you doing, Jane?"

"Good. Just trying to think of a less rock 'n' roll name than 'Osgood.'"

"Robert Zimmerman," Max answers.

"Who?"

Opening the grocery sack, Steve pulls out some gas station fried chicken and a large order of home fries. "Come on, you guys hungry?"

We eat around the cable spool. Max and Steve drink beer, me and Tyler have sweet tea. Steve wants to hear all about the catfish and last night.

"Where's her ring? Can I see it?"

Tyler shakes his head. "I must've left it on the houseboat. It sunk."

"This whole thing…" Steve finishes his fries, wiping his hands on his jeans. "The whole thing… just… whoa, you know?"

"Ever hear anything like it?" Tyler asks.

"Nuh-uh. I've seen the ghosts over at Forks of Cypress.

But they just looked like real pale light, nothing solid. But you know, the Devil's Circle is near the lake," Steve says. "Maybe that has something to do with all this."

Max shakes his head. "The Devil's Circle is way out, off of Wilson Highway."

Tyler says, "No, it's just past the embankment, real close to downtown. It's on private land, and the owners keep it quiet in case they ever want to sell."

Max keeps shaking his head. "I'm telling you, Twitchy went—" His phone rings, and he pulls it out. "Hey! How's it going? Where are you guys?" He carries the phone into the living room. The rest of us keep talking about ghosts.

Everybody knows the story of the Devil's Circle, even if nobody's sure where it is. Long ago, there was a kid who played banjo better than almost anybody around here. One night the Devil showed up to dance. The boy was too scared to stop playing, so he played all night while the Devil swirled around and around. Finally, the boy just collapsed from exhaustion. The next morning, he found a boot stuffed with money and a wide circle where nothing would grow. No animals would get close to it, not even the best-trained horses or hunting dogs. The boy never picked up the banjo again, and the Devil's Circle is still like that today.

The Forks of Cypress plantation house burned down a century ago. The great white columns still mark where it stood, though. Terrified ghosts still glimmer above the foundations some nights, and kids with cars dare each other to drive out there, rush up, and touch the columns.

We talk about Crybaby Bridge, the face in the Pickens

County Courthouse window, and Gabriel's Hounds tearing through the woods every Good Friday. They're just scraps of stories, told and retold, parts lost and patched up with spare parts from fairy tales and movies. I wonder if the people from the holler knew the truth about them—the people like Mattie Peake, who'd lived there before the dam, far away from town, down where nights were as black as sin and fevers disguised themselves as toads.

Just as LeighAnn comes home, Max reappears and kisses her. "Guess what? Against the Dawn are playing the Bandito Burrito on Thursday."

"Awesome!"

"That was Jessie on the phone. She wanted to know if they could crash here. I went ahead and said yes."

LeighAnn gives a thumbs-up. "Gonna be like college again, except we won't go to class the next morning. 'Course, we didn't go to class when we were in college, so it'll be like college again!"

"And also, she wanted us for their opening act."

LeighAnn sighs. "Oh, well. You tell her Patterson was gone?"

"Yeah, but—"

"Tyler can fill in," Steve says. Max and LeighAnn both look at Tyler.

Tyler shakes his head and concentrates on his chicken leg. "Come on, Ultimate, I told you, I'm not looking to be in a band right now."

"You're the only person who already knows all our songs."

"Barely. Not nearly as good as Patterson."

Max says, "How about you just stay for practice tonight, see how it goes?"

Tyler nods. "We'll see how it goes."

Ultimate Steve claps him on the back. LeighAnn goes to change out of her skirt suit. While she's in the bedroom, that sketchy girl who was hanging on Steve the other day appears—I didn't even hear the front door open. The first thing she does is hug Steve, pressing her face to his sweaty, mucky work shirt and breathing deep.

"Hey Britney. How's it going?"

"Hey, sweetness." She stands on her tip-toes to kiss him.

The guys head into the living room and start getting ready. Britney isn't in the band, so she just sits on the couch and plays with Steve's hair. LeighAnn returns, wearing cutoffs and a tee, no shoes. Microwaving a chicken thigh, she glances around the kitchen and says, "You cleaned."

"A little. Also, I walked the dogs."

"Great. Were they good boys?"

"Sure were."

"So you still feeling bad for calling me nasty names?" Her voice is calm, conversational, just like it was this morning.

"A little." My face starts burning, and I focus hard at the floor.

LeighAnn punches me in the chest, stepping into it like a pitcher. Icicles stab down to my elbows. They freeze muscles, and I can't get a breath. Clutching my chest, I drop to my knees on the freshly swept linoleum.

"How about now?" she asks.

"Think I'm over it," I croak.

"Awesome." The microwave dings. She gets her chicken, then steps over me. Walking into the living room, she yells, "All right! I'm feeling all Motörhead tonight. Let's set it off!"

They sit and stand in a half circle, starting with a song called "Catatonic State Marching Band." They play fast and loud, first Max singing, then everybody joining in more or less together. They make the window panes rattle in their frames, and I think I know why a neighbor took a baseball bat to their mailbox.

In between practicing the song, they sip beer, talk about other bands, and joke around, filling the night with laughter. Of course, while Tyler's playing, we're not doing anything to help you, Holly. We're not getting any closer to figuring out what's going on. I'm not any closer to getting to go home. Tyler will see his parents, sleep in his own bed tonight, so what does he care about me?

They start into the same song again. Ultimate Steve bangs his drums, sweat flying from his hair and beard. He holds his drumsticks with the scarred stump of his finger sticking out like he's sipping tea with the Queen of England.

What was that Banana Hammocks song, Holly? "Chainsaw Girl." No, "Chainsaw Heartbreak"? Something stupid like that. And then one time Steve decided to add a chainsaw solo, revving it in rhythm to the song. I bet the audience loved that right up until he cut off his finger.

The next day you told me about it. "Then he picks it up off the stage and just sticks it in the cooler." Your eyes were wide and all your words rushed together. "Just down in the ice with the drinks. Then he goes back and finishes the gig."

"Gross, gross! How could he do that? That's so gross."

"But he finished the gig! They did, like, four more songs, and Steve never missed a beat! He had blood running all down his—"

"Ew, don't tell me. Why didn't Tyler and them take him to the ER?"

"They did afterward, but it was too late. Doctor couldn't reattach it."

"So wait, if he'd gone to the ER right away, they could have?"

"Well, yeah. Maybe. But..." We stared at each other, neither understanding the other. We might as well have been speaking different languages. "Jane, he finished the gig! Just sticks it in the cooler and sits back down at his kit and counts off the next song. Blood running all down his arm, and he never missed a beat."

And somehow that made him a titan of rock, not a total lunatic. Somehow that made him the Ultimate Steve—all other Steves mere imitations. And somehow I wound up hiding here with these losers.

Quit, quit it. I'm being nice.

Still, the noise fills the whole house. It fills me, every *boom-cha-boom* rattling my bones. I wish he'd chopped off his whole hand, not just a finger.

Nice. Be nice.

After an hour or so, Stratofortress switches to a new song, "Poppy Red, Moth White." It's a twangy little song about a girl who never stays in any one place for long. Standing in the doorway, I watch Tyler's fingers on the strings. I watch Max's

Adam's apple quiver up and down as he sings; LeighAnn, her whole body swaying back and forth like a metronome.

The fear and frustration that have held me tight all day—the worry about you, about my parents—starts to slide away. There's something hypnotic about watching musicians play, following their small, certain motions as they find that groove. They carry you into the groove without you realizing it, without you really even wanting to. I look down and see I'm tapping my foot.

Remember all those afternoons I sat around and watched you practice, Holly? I thought we were just wasting time. If I was ever impatient with you, I'm sorry. Now? I'd give anything for one more hour, watching you pull music out of your pa-paw's rumbling old guitar.

The song they try next is called "Cheers." I sit on the couch beside Britney while Max pulls out a notebook with all his songs in it. The front is covered with pictures of angels drawn in ballpoint pen. He shows the chords to Tyler. When Tyler's ready, Steve marks time on his snare, and the others fall in. Just as Max opens his mouth to sing, though, Tyler hits the wrong chord. He corrects himself, but now he's off-time, tripping everybody else up.

"Sorry," he murmurs in the sudden quiet.

"No problem," Max says. "Just remember you have to drop to D after the intro."

Tyler nods. "I know, I just . . . sorry."

"No problem." Max points to Steve, and they start again. Then again.

Max takes Tyler's guitar from him and shows him the piece really slowly, then in the correct time, then they start again.

Then again. Under Tyler's fingers, the song flutters around with one broken wing.

"Tyler, come on, man." Peeling off his shirt, Steve mops his face with it. Everybody's tired. Everybody's hot. With the amps turned on—and the carpeted walls adding an extra layer of insulation—the heat sucks on us like candy.

"Sorr—"

"Stop." Max cuts him off, annoyed and trying not to show it. "Don't apologize. Just . . . it's back to A for the bridge."

"I know!"

"If you know, then do it!" Max yells.

"All right, everybody take five," LeighAnn says, pulling her guitar strap over her head.

"No. I want to get this," Tyler says.

"No," LeighAnn answered. "Take five, go get some water or something."

Tyler sets down his guitar without a word. I try to catch his eye, but he avoids my gaze and walks into the kitchen. I follow him and watch him fill a glass with tap water. I'm not sure what to say, but I know I have to say something.

"I'm having fun listening to you guys practice."

Tyler snorts. "You didn't hear me keep screwing up?"

"You got the first songs, no problem." I shrug.

"Those are easy, three and four easy chords. 'Cheers,' it's got an F barre chord, a bent note right before dropping into A. Then—"

I wave my hands and shake my head. "I don't know

anything about that, about bent bars or anything. I just know that I used to spend a lot of time listening to Holly practice, and, um, I've missed it. I didn't really even know how bad I missed it until tonight. So, you know, whatever happens with this one song or with you playing with Stratofortress, I've had fun tonight."

He gives me a fake rock-star grin and shoots a finger-gun at me. "Always looking out for the fans."

"Stop." I laugh and push his hand away. "And just, um, I was sort of a B-word yesterday, when I got mad at you for wanting to come by here. But I'm really glad Steve called you after Holly died. And I'm really glad they kept you playing music. They're pretty good friends."

Tyler wraps an arm around my middle and heaves me off my feet, squeezing me against his bulk in a one-armed bear hug.

"Ack! You're all sweaty! Let go, let go!"

Complaining only makes him plant a fat kiss on my cheek before dropping me back down and heading into the living room. At least he seems more confident as he slips his guitar back over his head. Steve counts them off again. The song rises and collapses again. Rise and collapse. Rise and collapse. Rise and ... rise! Notes scuttle up the walls like blue-tailed skinks. Britney squeezes my hand. Her feet drum to the beat. My heart thumps to it.

The song falls apart, but we've seen how good it can be. "Yay, guys!" Britney cheers. "You're so close!" Everybody's hungry for it now, despite the sludgy heat.

Steve launches into the now-familiar intro. Rise and collapse. Rise and … rise … and rise … Holly, they've got it!

Frog-slick with sweat, Max sings and bobs to the sound; he knows they've got it this time. Tyler bounces along the rhythm Max lays down, pushing and pulling against it. I'm dancing with Britney. We have to dance or we'll explode.

The last chord shivers to silence, then everybody shrieks, wild and wordless. We rush Tyler. Britney kisses him, and I hug his neck. The three members of Stratofortress lean together for a few seconds, then straighten up. Max says, "All right Tyler, we need a rhythm guitar for Thursday, and you need somewhere for your girlfriend to stay."

"Girlfriend? No, Jane's not my—"

"I'm not his girlfriend."

Max rolls his eyes. "Whatever. But if you want us to help you, you've got to help us. So either you're in the band, or we sell her to a Saudi prince's pleasure dome."

I blush pink, but Tyler just snickers. "Fine, fine. I'll play."

There are fist-bumps all around. LeighAnn leaves to get more beer. Everybody's exhausted—even me and Britney somehow. I step out onto the back patio for some fresh air. The summer night feels like temptation itself. The air is as hot as tangled sheets. It smells like magnolia and honeysuckle, like sweet boys just vanished into the dark. Stratofortress's song is still rattling around behind my breastbone. Even in the quiet, I can feel its rhythm in there, in place of my busted-watch heart. By the time Tyler comes out and sits down beside me, the song has almost faded away. But I'm still smiling, really smiling for the first time in a month.

"Thanks," he says. "For that pep talk back there."

I shrug, twisting my bare toes into the cool dust. "Didn't say anything that wasn't true."

"So tomorrow, want to go look for this Mattie Peake? I mean, Decatur isn't that big a town. We might get lucky and find somebody who knows her."

"Sure." I nod, not bothering to mention that it's still a Hail Mary play.

"And listen. I've got some money saved up. Why don't you take it." Opening his wallet, Tyler pulls out several twenties.

"No. Thanks, but I'm okay."

He persists. "It's not a big deal. It's money my grand-mother sent me for my birthday."

"No. I don't need it." I push his hand away. I could use the money, but I'm embarrassed to take it.

"Jane. We're in this together. Whatever I can do to help you, I'm going to do it."

"Then..." My hand is still on top of his. His skin is like soft leather, but the muscles underneath are as hard as steel cable. I trace the callouses at the tips of Tyler's fingers. I want him to help me be happy again, Holly, even if it's just a few minutes at a time. I want to feel my heart beating again. "Then teach me to play guitar."

"S-Seriously?"

"Yeah. Will you teach me?"

"Like right now?"

"Right now."

He shrugs and puts the money away, saying, "Sure. You got it."

Thirteen

"Can we take this stuff outside? It's like a furnace in here."

"Sure, just unplug that amp. Be careful, it's heavy."

Isn't it kinda weird if you think about it, Holly? All those years hanging out with you, and I never learned to play music.

I goofed around with your guitar sometimes, but I never had any time to really learn how to play. There was always too much other stuff to do—church projects, youth group stuff, looking after my brothers and Faye. Besides, I had you. You knew all the songs I could ever want—the rejoicing ones, the gentle ones, the ones pulpy and wet with raw life.

I lug the amp out of the living room. Behind me, Tyler is winding cords around his arm. Max appears in the archway. "Um, you guys robbing us?"

"Jane wants to learn to play."

"Seriously?" Leaning out the window, Max shouts down the street. "LeighAnn! Jane wants to play guitar!"

"Really?" She starts jogging up the block with a six-pack of beer in each hand. "Give me a second. Don't let her start yet."

Suddenly, I'm plagued by experts.

"Here, cinch this up; your arms are shorter than Tyler's." Max tightens the guitar strap while Tyler worries with the little knobs. The light on the back patio has burned out, so there's just a string of old Halloween lights to see by—cheap plastic skulls grin down at us.

When Ultimate Steve plugs the amp in, the guitar comes alive, humming, trembling gently against my stomach. I jerk my hand away from the strings, and LeighAnn laughs at me. "Relax, it won't bite." She sits in the grass, leaning back on one elbow, beer in the other hand.

Unwinding my grimy bandage, I flex my sweat-soft fingers. "Okay, what should I learn first?"

"Freebird! Whoo!" Britney shouts.

"'Mary Had a Little Lamb' is kinda the universal first song," LeighAnn says.

"'Mary Had a . . .'" I roll my eyes, "Come on, that's lame. Even I know that's lame."

Max balks. "Have you ever heard Stevie Ray Vaughn's version of 'Mary Had a Little Lamb'? It's baller. It's so baller, it's banned in, like, sixteen countries."

"Nuh-uh."

"Right hand to God. Banned in all those Islamic countries 'cause women kept ripping off their burkas and going nuts." As Max talks, he presses a thin black pick into my hand and bends my fingers to the frets. It makes me wince; my hand and arm are still covered in scabs from where you grabbed me. "Okay, just strum all the strings, and that's a G chord," Tyler says.

I strum the strings. Notes fall thick and flat or buzz strangely. Everybody groans. "What was that? Come on." The experts swarm again.

"Don't go straight down with the pick. And stiffen your wrist up."

"Here. Don't let your fingertips touch the other strings; that's where that buzzing came from."

"Don't grab the neck like a baseball bat. You want to almost be cupping it in the palm of your hand."

"Yeah, hold it like a little baby bunny."

"Okay, okay. Let me try." Maybe this was a bad idea, but I shoo them back for a second try. Biting my bottom lip, I squeeze the strings against the frets and strum.

The chord comes like bottled thunder, knocking the wind out of me. It startles Hobbit and Cookie. They begin to bark frantically. Stratofortress cheers, and by the time Hobbit and Cookie calm down, other dogs in other yards have picked up their panic, filling the neighborhood with howls. The racket spreads across the night like ripples across water.

Everyone hoots and laughs. I clap my hands over my mouth as hiccupy giggles bubble up. I'd forgotten how much fun it was to be so loud.

Fourteen

G…D seven…G…G…D seven… Max's acoustic guitar in my lap, bare feet tucked under me, I work through the chords for "Mary Had a Little Lamb."

I woke up before dawn, Holly, and my head immediately filled with worries about you, worries about my family. I knew I wouldn't get back to sleep without my Tenex, so I decided to practice instead.

G…D seven…G…G…D seven…

Max and Ultimate Steve wake up and leave for work. In the master bedroom, LeighAnn's alarm clock goes off. I hear her cuss and slap the snooze button.

G…D seven…G…G…D seven…

Alarm. Cuss. Slap.

G…D seven…G…G…D seven…

Alarm. Cuss. Slap.

G…D seven…G…G…D seven…

Alarm. Cuss. Something smacks against the wall. A few minutes later, I hear the shower running.

G... D seven... G... G... D seven...

LeighAnn shuffles down the hall, mostly dressed, no makeup. I look up and smile. "Good morning."

"You still here?"

"I made coffee."

LeighAnn nods and disappears into the kitchen.

G... D seven... G... G... D seven...

LeighAnn reappears with a coffee cup. She's shaking her head. "You're hitting that G wrong. You have to arch your middle finger more." Still bleary eyed from not enough sleep, she yanks my finger into position. "There. Now press down as hard as you can."

I press down past the point where the steel string hurts my fingertip. *G... D seven... G... G... D seven...*

"Better, better, but look, put your fingers here and here."

"Ow! Stop!" I jerk away. "Fingers don't bend like that."

"Sure they do." Pressing her left fingertips against her right palm, she bends them so far back it makes me a little queasy. "Just have to stretch the ligaments more."

"But it hurts."

"Supposed to hurt at first. You're not doing it right if it doesn't hurt."

"It hurts up in my biceps. How is that even possible?" Shaking cramps out of my fingers, I try again.

"Good. There you go." She starts putting her earrings in. "So you have any plans today?"

"Me and Tyler are going to look for a woman, an old root-worker who may know something about Holly."

"Cool." LeighAnn sips her coffee. I flex my fingers, working out some of the soreness from bending them in strange ways.

The silence starts growing uncomfortable. I try to think of something to crack it. "So, where'd you learn to play music?"

"Muscle Shoals High Marching Band."

I perk up and grin. "Seriously? Just the regular high school band?"

"Yeah. I played clarinet."

"I figured it be something more rock 'n' roll, like Tighty-Whitey and the Banana Hammocks."

LeighAnn rolls her eyes. "Only Ultimate could come up with something like that. He's so gross."

"So how'd you go from clarinet to bass guitar?"

"Well, I was in the marching band, but I really wanted to be in jazz ensemble, right?" She straightens up, eager to tell the story. "But all the clarinet chairs were taken up by seniors, and they always got preference. So I borrowed a friend's bass, holed up in my room for the summer, and taught myself to play."

"Awesome. And now you're a big rock star."

"Whatever. I'm a bank teller with half a psychology degree."

"Hey, I've see your flyers in the hall. You're doing real shows and stuff."

"You see the one that says 'Stradivarius'?"

"Okay, but still, you're doing something you love, right? And it's something nobody else ever could. I mean, even if somebody else played the same song, it could never sound exactly like how you play it." I'm remembering what your papaw told me.

"Yeah. I suppose."

"No, it's true. Before Holly died, I never really thought about how much dies with somebody. I mean, I'll never hear Holly play again. Or how she laughed or anything. It's hard... thinking about all the stuff that's gone."

LeighAnn nods but doesn't say anything else. I think maybe I've gotten too personal. As the silence around us hardens again, she says, "You know, I heard Holly play. She was really good."

"Really? When?"

"Tyler brought over a recording of her playing at your church. 'Everybody Hurts,' that R.E.M. song, and uh, 'More to This Life.' Seriously. She was great."

"Thanks. That means a lot." And it does. LeighAnn wouldn't say it unless she meant it.

LeighAnn finishes getting dressed. Grabbing her makeup to put on in the car, she says, "Hey, be careful looking for that root-worker, okay?"

"I will." I guess we're friends now. At least in the sense that LeighAnn doesn't wish me dead.

"And make sure Tyler's back here by five thirty. We've got to practice for the show tomorrow."

"Five thirty. We'll be here."

She throws the devil's horn sign as she heads out the door. I try to play some more, but my hand has cramped up so bad I can't. Instead, I kneel down and pray. I ask

God to comfort my family, but I don't really believe anymore that He's listening. He's pulled His hand away from us. He's left us in the wilderness and won't even say why.

These days, praying just makes me angrier. So I get back to my feet and go walk the dogs. We go all the way to Tennessee Street this time. Hobbit stops to sniff every tree and crack in the sidewalk. Cookie strains at his leash, always wanting to go faster.

Still waiting for Tyler to find a way to skip school, I move the laundry from the washing machine to the dryer, straighten up the living room, and polish Steve's drum kit until I can see myself in his cymbals.

When Tyler finally shows up, he has a bag of jelly doughnuts. They make me realize how hungry I am. While I scarf them down, Tyler says, "So, Brooke called me last night."

"Oh?"

"Yeah. She's started a prayer circle for you. She's really worried about you."

I snort. "That's just her way of gossiping without feeling bad about it." Everybody in the youth group must know I ran away by now. I bet they're just loving how I finally snapped. My face burns with embarrassment. I want to scream and yank Brooke's stupid hair. But that won't help you, Holly, so I grab Max's guitar instead. "Come on, let's go."

Tyler asks, "You're taking the guitar?"

"Yeah. You drive, I practice." Just holding it makes me feel better, just knowing I can make the guitar shout for me.

Decatur is upriver from Florence, far away from the dam and lake. Tyler drives past cotton fields, troops of blackbirds watching us from power lines, and houses clinging to Highway 31 like dew on spider silk. I sit in the passenger seat and play "Mary Had a Little Lamb."

Despite the soreness in my fingers, my hand skims across the strings like a water strider. Holly, can you see? Even with a few buzzing notes, the little tune comes through. The string bites right into the blister on my ring finger and I wince, almost yelp. The song shivers to silence.

"Coming along." Tyler nods. We cross a bridge into downtown Decatur. Swinging into the library parking lot, Tyler says, "Here we go. They must have a phone book."

They loan us a phone book, but the only Peake is Peake Landscaping. When Tyler calls the number, a man with a Spanish accent tells him he bought the company from James Peake eleven years ago, and no, he doesn't know where James is now.

Sighing, Tyler says, "Well, let's look around. If she was as well-known as you say, maybe somebody remembers her."

Downtown, restaurants and gift shops have moved into old brick warehouses and the train depot. A little bell chimes over the door when we walk into Sweetie Cakes Bakery. The air inside is cool and chocolate-scented.

A woman in an apron is laying out trays of cookies. "Hi. Can I help you?"

"Maybe." I smile wide. "We're looking for a woman named Mattie Peake."

"Sorry, no Matties work here."

I nod and keep smiling. "Right, but we think she lived around here once. Some people might have called her Auntie Peake."

The woman shakes her head. "Sorry."

"She was a, uh, root-worker."

"A what, honey?"

"She mixed up medicines and, like, charms maybe."

"I don't know any root-workers. Y'all need to buy something or get on out."

It's the mark of a good Southern upbringing when a woman can make it clear she doesn't like you and may call the cops while still keeping her voice as bright as birdsong. We thank her and leave.

We're run out of Momma's Kountry Kitchen and the Ooh-La-La Gift Shop just as quickly. The guy at Excalibur Vintage and Vinyl thinks we're playing some joke on him. The man in the Chevron gas station lifts his eyes to the ceiling and scratches his chin. "Hmm . . . don't think I know any Peakes. Sorry."

"She was a root-worker," Tyler says. "She knew how to make charms and medicines and things."

The man scowls. "Sounds like some sorta witch."

"Well, yeah. But she didn't curse people or anything. She was good. She helped people when they were sick and stuff."

"No such thing as a good witch. They all get their power from the devil, and their power is nothing but tricks. You kids might know that if you got your tails to church."

"Okay. Sorry to bother you." Tyler turns to leave, but I can't.

"We go to church," I say.

"Yeah?" He snorts. "Must not be a *real* church if you're out looking for witches."

"Come on, Jane." Tyler plucks at my sleeve.

"We're trying to help somebody. You don't know—"

"All I need to know is the word of the Lord, little girl. 'There shall not be found among you any who practice magic, call on evil spirits for aid, be a fortune-teller, or call forth the spirits of the dead.'"

"No! This isn't—we're not—we're trying to help somebody."

But the man shakes his head sadly and won't look at me. Tyler has my wrist now. "Forget it, Jane. Jane, let's go."

We leave. The man's voice chases us out the door. "It's not too late. 'Though your sins are like scarlet, they can be made white as snow.'"

Stepping back out under the sun's hard glare, Tyler says, "Forget it. Don't worry about it, okay?"

I'm too mad to say anything. Shaking my head, I just climb into the truck.

"Jane...come on."

"I hate this, Tyler."

"I know."

"I hate not being able to go to church. I hate Brooke gossiping and who knows what everybody else thinks about me. I hate not knowing if this is right or not." And I hate praying and feeling like no one's listening, but I keep that part to myself.

"It's right. We're helping Holly, Jane. In your heart, you know it's the right thing to do."

"I don't know anything! Everything's messed up. Everything's all wrong. I just want to go home."

"We're going to get you home."

If I could just cry, I'd feel better. But all my sadness and frustration keep building up as heat in the back of my neck, an aching pulse right behind my eye, and I can't let it go. It just keeps building and building so I can't think, can't even see straight.

I grab Max's guitar. I push some of the frustration down my fingertips, down into *G... D seven... G... G...*

Tyler keeps talking. "Besides, we're not trying to 'call forth the spirits of the dead.' We're trying to put Holly's spirit to rest. We're just trying to put things right. And Mattie—"

"Ow! Errrgh!" My blister tears open on one of the guitar strings. I clench my hand to my chest, feeling oily fluid leak between my fingers. "Ow, ow, owww!"

"Blister pop?" Tyler grins.

"Oh, I can't look. You have a Band-Aid in here?"

"No, no, can't let it heal. You have to keep playing until it hardens into a callous."

"I'm bleeding, Tyler. I can't play, it hurts!"

"I know it hurts. Look." He shows me his hand. Shiny, crescent-shaped scars crown each finger pad. "But if you stop practicing now, let it heal up, it'll just blister and pop all over again. You have to keep playing. Let it hurt, let it bleed, let your fingers toughen up."

I lift the guitar onto my thigh again. Touching the strings, I wince, then shake my hand and blow on it. "Guess the one on my ring finger is going to pop too?"

"Yep."

I set my fingers back on the strings. *G... D seven... G... G...* I won't give up; I don't care. Clenching my teeth, I let anger push me through the pain. My bloody-gummy fingers smear the strings black.

"Good, good. So, you want to call it a day?" Tyler asks.

I shake my head, still hunched over the guitar, still playing. "We're here. We do this." Each note stings like a fire-ant bite, but I won't stop. Holly, do you see me? I don't care how much it hurts, I don't care what we have to do. I won't stop until we've saved you.

Life is supposed to hurt. You're not doing it right if it doesn't hurt.

That thought keeps me going as we get back to it, asking about Mattie Peake, people thinking we're crazy or going to Hell or both. Under every sour stare, I squeeze my fingers into a fist, stroking my grimy blister like the pearl of great price. Blessed are the stubborn, for sooner or later, they shall inherit the earth.

It's past lunchtime when Tyler yelps, "Penn's!" and breaks away across the street. The restaurant sign reads *C. F. Penn's Hamburgers* in neon letters.

"Ever have a Penn's burger?" Tyler asks after I catch up.

"Uh-uh. Are they good?"

"My dad took me here sometimes, back when he owned that apartment building out here. Come on, I'm buying."

I follow his wide strides. "So are they good?"

"They're ... kind of an acquired taste, but come on. This place has been around forever, so we should ask them about Mattie Peake anyway."

The door is propped open to let in a breeze, but the air inside still feels oily. A couple of flies wander across the patched vinyl booths. The waitress and cook both look skinny and scorched dark, like burned french fries.

We climb onto stools at the counter. The waitress smiles. "What can I get you?"

"Give us two double cheeseburgers with the works—"

"Uh, just a single for me."

"Sure?" Tyler asks.

I nod.

"Okay. One double, one single. The works on both. And onion rings and Cokes." Tyler swivels on his stool.

"Got it." The waitress calls out our ticket to the cook. Taking three patties from an under-the-counter fridge, he drops them into the seething oil of the fryer.

"He's deep fat frying our burgers?" I hiss to Tyler.

"Give it a try. You'll like it."

The "works" are mustard, tomato, and lettuce. The bun tastes buttery from the grease, and the whole thing sort of dissolves in my mouth and slithers down my throat. I take two bites, and I'm done. At least the Coke is cool and sweet.

The waitress heads for the door with a cigarette in her hand. As she passes by, I say, "Excuse me. We were wondering, do you know anybody named Mattie Peake?"

She twiddles the cigarette between her fingers. "Don't think so. Sorry."

"She could mix up medicines and things. People might have said she was sort of a witch, but—"

"Auntie Peake ain't no witch." The cook turns, glaring at us. "She's a root-worker."

Tyler tries to talk and sputters on his drink. I ask, "You know her? You know how we can find to her?"

"She mixed up medicines for folks the doctor couldn't help. She never cursed anybody. Ms. Peake broke the curses witches put on people."

"Well, it seems like people don't really see the difference between root-workers and witches anymore."

Scraping the grill with his spatula, he snorts. "Witches get their power from the devil. Root-workers get theirs from the Lord up in Heaven. I'd say that's a big difference."

"Yes, sir. Absolutely."

"My parents, their first three babies all died before they were a week old. Broke my mamma's heart so it never healed again. The doctor said she was just too frail to have babies, but she went to Auntie Peake, and Auntie Peake saw there was a curse on my mamma. An ex-girlfriend of my dad's had put it on her when they got married. But Auntie Peake broke it, and I'm living, breathing proof that Ms. Mattie Peake never did anything but good for any soul. Don't come into this place calling Auntie Peake a witch. My people owe her too much to let that stand."

"I'm sorry. But do you know how we can find her? Please, we have to talk to her."

"Oh yeah? What about?" He turns all the way around for the first time, glancing from Tyler to me with suspicious eyes.

Tyler says, "It's our friend. She drowned and became a ghost, and we need to put her to rest, but we need somebody who knows about these things to help us."

In the clear light of day, it still sounds unbelievable to me.

But the cook just nods, wiping his hands on his splotched apron. "Auntie Peake had a stroke, something like that, few years back. I heard they put her in Morningside."

"Morningside?"

"The nursing home out on 31," he adds.

"Thank you! You don't know how much you've helped us."

After Tyler finishes lunch, we step back out into the noon-time heat. I say, "I don't even want to know what that burger is gonna do to your guts later."

"That's why you get the cheese, see? The cheese is like a parachute. It creates drag and slows the meat down as it hurls through your colon."

"Tyler! Ew!"

He chuckles and shakes his head. "So you feel better now? Now that we're clear Auntie Peake is a root-worker, not a witch?"

"I just want to know if this will work. I don't care what she's called if she can help Holly."

Morningside has cinder-block walls painted half yellow and half white. It smells like Ajax and pee. After we sign in, the nurse points us down the hall. Auntie Peake sits in bed with her slippers on. She doesn't look like much of a witch or root-worker or anything at all. One arm is shrunken and twisted from the stroke. Her body curves toward her strong side. Her roommate watches TV, but Auntie Peake ignores it.

"Ms. Peake? I'm Tyler. This is Jane, and uh, we need your help."

"Get my glasses. On the table there."

Tyler fetches her tortoiseshell glasses from the cluttered

bedside table. She puts them on and studies us. Her eyes blink rapidly against the thick lenses—moths fluttering inside mason jars.

"Get my water there."

Tyler hands her a cup of water with a bendy straw in it. "It's my girlfriend, Holly. She drowned this spring. Drowned in Wilson Lake. And she's become some sort of a ghost. It's like she's trapped in the lake."

"I heard that you knew about another ghost," I say, butting in. "Somebody named Tommy Mud-and-Sticks. We think Holly's turned into something like him."

Auntie Peake closes her eyes. "Poor, poor Tommy. That was the last winter before they built the dam and flooded us out of the holler. Old Amos Buckley had a devil of a time tracking him down and putting him to rest. 'Course, people love telling a good haunt story, especially after somebody got the notion that he only haunted the prettiest girls." She grunts disapprovingly. "Vain little things all over Lauderdale County started swearing he'd come up, chased them 'round, for years after he was gone."

It takes effort for her to hand the cup back to Tyler. Setting it down, Tyler says, "Amos Buckley. He helped Holly's grandfather, actually. He was really sick, and Mr. Buckley found a fever disguised as a frog in his house."

"Uh-huh. Old Amos was hard as a nail but twice as sharp. Won't be any more root-workers like him again."

"Do you know how he got rid of Tommy?"

"Same as any restless spirit, I imagine. Most aren't wicked, they just gets lost. Happens sometimes when people drown in the river."

"How come?"

Auntie Peake's good shoulder shrugs. "The river has its own way of things."

"You mean, like, it's alive? It has a soul?"

"Only man has an eternal soul, young lady, only man can leave Earth to enter Paradise. But sometimes things of this earth—old, old things like rivers—they grow some power akin to a soul, something that makes them more than what you can see with your eyes or hold in your hands."

"How?" I ask.

She shrugs again. "Rivers are strange. They're not human places like towns. A human's soul gets tangled up in the river's power, it can be dangerous pulling them out again."

"We know. We already called her once and . . . it doesn't matter. We have to do it."

Auntie Peake doesn't ask what I mean. She sends me to the nurses station for a pen and paper. When I come back, she starts to write while explaining. "First, you have to find your friend, the part of the river that's shaped like her. The body won't be *her* body anymore, but her soul is still holding it together."

I remember the clay-skinned thing that crawled onto the boat and spoke with your voice. I shudder, realizing we'll have to face it again.

Auntie Peake goes on. "Next, mix together white chalk and slaked lime and draw a circle around yourselves. No spirits can step into the circle, so you'll be safe. Then pray over her. Call down Heaven's blessing using this prayer here." She hands me back the scratch paper. The lines cramp up along the right-hand margin. They read, *Lord, guide this troubled soul to rest. Carry her from darkness and cold evermore, for those washed clean in Your blood shall fear not. Amen.*

I touch the words. *Fear not.*

"Holly's motto."

Tyler asks, "Huh?"

"Fear not. Remember? She painted it on her guitar."

"Oh yeah. Yeah. See?"

I nod. We're on the right path. This will work. It has to. "Thank you so much," I say to Auntie Peake.

"That all you came for?"

"Yeah, I...I guess." A twinge of guilt makes me squirm; we're taking what we need from her and just leaving her here. It's not right. But we're so close.

Guilt hits Tyler at the same moment. He stammers, "Anything we can do for you before we go?"

She thinks for a moment, then, "What's the milkweed like?"

"What?"

"The milkweed. Out in the fields, out by the roads."

"It's all over. It's everywhere."

"This late in the summer? Hmm... going to be a long, wet winter."

We spend another half-hour telling her about the wild-flowers and hummingbirds and pawpaw trees. Auntie Peake reads them all as weather signs for the coming year. I feel sorry for her, a root-worker cut off from the land, with just a window looking out onto a nursing home courtyard.

Still, I'm anxious to go. I fold the prayer she wrote out into tight little squares. Then I unfold it, then fold it back. I want to get this over with, Holly.

"What about foxfire? There been a lot of foxfire this summer?"

"Um, I don't think so. Haven't heard anything, at least."

She nods. "When people start seeing foxfire lights every night, especially in the graveyards, it'll mean the Lord is coming. The time of Revelation is at hand. We'll have days then, maybe weeks, but not more."

We finally leave and drive to Home Depot. Slaked lime comes in big ten-gallon buckets. The only powdered chalk they have is electric blue, but we find sticks of white sidewalk chalk we can crush up. Since the lime is caustic, I get heavy-duty rubber gloves too. We carry everything out to Tyler's truck and head out to Swallow's Nest Bluff.

Holly, don't you remember the ice storm when we were ten? Power lines were down all over the city, but you came and stayed with us because we at least had propane for heat. There was no TV, no computers, nothing. We spent hours just walking around the neighborhood, seeing the snow cover everything. We walked over to Swallow's Nest Bluff. It looked so different from how we'd ever seen it before. The lake had a white crust of ice, and the blackberry bushes were leafless, brown, and curled up asleep. The storm had sheathed every branch of every pine, and every needle of every branch, in clear ice. When the wind blew, they jingled together like thousands of tiny bells.

How can I be the only person left who remembers that day, Holly?

Tyler pulls over near the bluff. Nobody is around, so we get to work. I take a chunk of limestone and use it to grind the chalk into powder on the truck's tailgate. We haven't been to the river since we came with your pa-paw. I think about him, and my stomach tightens into a knot. My hands shake. I drop one of the chalk sticks, and it rolls into the weeds. "Son of a biscuit!"

"Jane, relax." Tyler touches my shoulder, making me jump. I punch him in the arm. He just laughs. "Relax. I know you're nervous. Me too. But if we do this right, we'll put Holly to rest and you can go home. Just focus on that. Going home, okay?"

The thought is a cicada in my chest, light and buzzing. I might be holding Faye—tickling her, smelling her sweet skin—in a couple hours. I'm gonna squeeze her so hard her head might pop off.

I take some deep breaths and steady myself. We're here for you, Holly. We're going to put you to rest. We're going to make sure you don't hurt anybody else. I find the stray chalk stick and grind it to powder. We fill one of the bags with the lime and chalk. Tyler slings Max's guitar over his shoulder, and then we sidle between the blackberry bushes. The water winks orange between the pines. The tire swing turns slowly, looking for all the world like a noose. We walk past it, creeping down the steep slope of the bank, getting as close to the water as we dare.

Mud-crusted turtles bask on a half-submerged log. When we get close, they slide into the green water, *splish, splish-splish*, then everything falls quiet again. Suddenly, Tyler stops and stares, then picks a white piece of trash out of the wildflowers. "Jane, check it out."

It's a water-splotched photograph, wrinkled and peeling. But I can still make out the grinning face of your me-maw.

"This must be one of the pictures Mr. Alton had on the houseboat," Tyler says. "It must have floated up from the wreckage, and the wind blew it up here."

I nod. Is this a good omen or a bad one, Holly? It doesn't matter. Tyler can't just drop the picture back onto the ground, so he trudges back up to put it in his truck.

Waiting for him to come back, I take two fistfuls of the lime-and-chalk mixture in my gloved hands and draw a thin line of white powder around us. "Think it matters if it's not a perfect circle?" I ask when he reappears through the blackberry bushes.

"Probably not. Just make sure there aren't any gaps. Actually, go around twice to make sure."

After I draw another wide circle across the rocks and earth, Tyler starts playing "The Drowned Forest." Shielding my eyes with my hand, I stare out across the lake. Tyler's sad little melody still makes my chest ache, but I think about Faye, keep myself together, and keep watch.

The heat sags my shoulders like an old mattress. I smack at bugs and would love to dip my face in the water. Instead, I pace the inside of our white chalk border. I worry at the paper with Auntie Peake's prayer until it hangs limp with sweat from my palms. I borrow Tyler's Aviators so I can see better, but besides the bugs and boats zipping along in the distance, the world lies still.

Everything is still.

I squint up into the face of the bluff, up at the mud nests dotting the limestone. When I walk closer, Tyler stops playing. "Jane? Hey, don't cross the circle, Jane."

"The swallows are gone."

"Huh?"

"All the swallows. They're gone."

Tyler leaves the circle to walk up beside me. "Probably asleep. They feed mostly in the mornings and evenings."

I whip a stone at one of the nests. The wad of mud and dry grass comes spinning down, trailing a few downy feathers. No angry squawks, though. No rustle of wings from any of the nearby nests.

"Well." Tyler shrugs again. "When do they migrate?"

"Not this early. Something's wrong."

"What?"

"I don't know, but it's weird, isn't it?"

He pushes sweat-damp hair back. "I bet Holly scared them away. Animals maybe knew somehow she wasn't . . . you know, she wasn't right."

"She sent that catfish. Why would the swallows fly away when that catfish is doing what she tells it? And the plants aren't growing like last time. Remember the milfoil?"

"Yeah, but . . . I don't know. I don't know about catfish or stupid swallows or seaweed. I don't know what they meant when they were here, and I don't know what it means that they're not here."

Nudging the fallen nest with my toe, I say, "Just weird is all."

"What isn't weird anymore, Jane? C'mon, let's stick to the plan. Let's get back in the circle, okay? She might come any second."

So Tyler steps back into the magic circle and plays the song again. I sit down beside him and keep watch, but you're not coming, are you, Holly?

When Tyler finally gives up, I say, "Maybe she doesn't trust us anymore, after last time."

"Then let's just say the prayer."

"But Auntie Peake said we had to pray over Holly."

Tyler slumps down. "Well, what then?"

"We have to be patient. She's lost. She's scared. We were here once and—in her mind at least—we ran away from her. We have to keep playing, show her she can still trust us."

After another minute of rest, Tyler stands up again and keeps playing. He plays to the sinking sun. He plays while our stomachs cramp from hunger, and after my skin feels gritty and gross with dirt and sweat. Our protective circle has almost blown away. Finally, he sets the guitar down and says, "I don't think she's coming, Jane."

"What time is it?"

"Ten after five."

I sigh. I promised LeighAnn I'd have Tyler back for band practice at five thirty. As much as I hate leaving, it's pretty clear nothing is going to happen here tonight. "We'll come back tomorrow."

"Jane, I—"

"And the next day and the next day. As long as it takes until she knows she can trust us again." The words hurt. I want to hold Faye. I want to hear Yuri's laugh and sleep in my own bed. I want to go home tonight, and as I say the words, I feel that hope drift away like a dandelion seed. But it doesn't matter, Holly. I offer my pain up to you, a sign of my devotion.

Fifteen

Back at Stratofortress's house, I show the band my torn blister. I show I can still play through the pain. They all grin, and Max claps me on the shoulder. And I'm grinning too, even though it's stupid.

But you know what, Holly? I sort of get why you were impressed with Ultimate Steve that night he cut off his finger and finished the gig. Sometimes there's nothing keeping us going except mule-headed cussedness. It's not pretty, but it's respectable.

Then everything changes in an instant. Stratofortress gets ready for practice. Ultimate Steve sits down behind his drum kit, then whips around to look at me. "What... what did you do?"

"Nothing." I sit on the couch beside Britney. "What are you talking about?"

He tips one of the cymbals toward me, light from the

ceiling fan reflecting off its bright yellow surface. "You cleaned them."

"Well, yeah. Just...so?" I can feel everybody staring at me.

"How?" Steve snaps. "What did you do to them?"

"Nothing! I shined them a little. Vinegar and, and aluminum foil."

I glance at Tyler for support. Tyler tugs on his hair and says, "Jane, we have a gig tomorrow! Tomorrow!"

"So what? They'll look nice for the show now."

"They're not supposed to look *nice*!" Steve yells, twisting the word "nice" into a barbed fishhook. "They're supposed to look like crap. That's how you know they sound good. They're supposed to look scuffed and scratched from every song they've ever played. You clean them, you mess with their mojo."

"Their huh?"

"Mojo! Their magic." Leaning close, he taps the cymbals with his drumstick, then pushes the pedal that makes the two little ones clap together. "These aren't pots and pans, okay? I've had these cymbals since I was sixteen. I traded my entire comic book collection for them, everything, even my Wolverine and Deadpool stuff, like my entire childhood for them."

"But I didn't do any—"

Steve cuts me off. "I've played them every day since then. My sweat is in these things. My blood is in these things. That gives them mojo. That makes them more than what you can see or hold."

I start. It's almost exactly how Auntie Peake described the river earlier today. "I...I'm sorry," I mumble. "I didn't know."

"They still sound all right," LeighAnn says. "Come on, Ultimate."

"They're not all right! The overtones are thinner now, listen." He keeps tapping the cymbal.

Max says, "Come on, Ultimate, we have to get 'Cheers' down tonight."

Ultimate Steve straightens up, but he's still not happy. "Spend years getting them sounding just right, years pouring my heart and soul into them, but sure, stick them in the dishwasher. They'll be fine."

I decide to make myself scarce during practice, so I take Max's acoustic out onto the back patio. I try to play, but my hand is cramped into a claw. Instead, I listen to the band and turn the guitar over and over. Its top is blond wood, and the reflection of the plastic skull lights overhead wobbles across its surface.

Of course instruments have mojo. It's plain as day once you really think. The guitar is just wood and steel wires and empty holes. It's mostly just air. But you used a guitar to fill people with joy, drop them to their knees as quick as any rifle. Of course instruments are magical, of course they're more than what you can see and hold.

And of course the river has its own mojo. We've felt it before, Holly, swinging out over Swallow's Nest Bluff. And that winter afternoon when the frozen pines sang in the crisp, clean air. And all those fishing trips in Dad's boat, the never-still surface of the lake rising and dipping like the chest of sleeping Leviathan. Those waters have a deep, slow, quiet power older than any human soul. We've always known that, we just never had a name for it.

I don't notice the band taking a break until the glass door slides open and LeighAnn steps out, cigarette in hand. She says, "Hey. Doing okay?"

I nod and force a smile. "Steve still mad?"

"Oh, yeah. He'd burn your house down if you weren't staying here." She sits on the concrete steps beside me and whistles. Her dogs trot up to get petted. "Don't worry, though. He'll get over it."

"You guys are sounding better tonight."

She shrugs. "It's coming together, coming together. Now you're coming to the show tomorrow, right? Even if we totally bomb—"

"You're not going to bomb."

"Even if we bomb, Against the Dawn is amazing. Jessie, the singer, we were in a band together back in college. She pulled Against the Dawn together, like, a year ago after moving down to Atlanta, and they've already got a record contract."

"Wow. That's cool."

"Yeah, they're not huge yet or anything, but if this tour goes well, they really could be. You like ... what kind of music do you like, anyway?"

"Contemporary Christian. Mostly Christian rock."

"Oh."

"What?"

"Nothing. Just, 'Oh, okay. That's the music you like.'"

"Nuh-uh, that wasn't an understanding 'Oh.' That was a

sympathy 'Oh.' Like the 'Oh' you give somebody after their grandma dies. That 'Oh' was dangerously close to an 'Aw.'"

She's grinning. "It was just an 'Oh.'"

"Not all Christian stuff is lame. I mean, some of it is, but there are lots of bands that are really good."

"I like some of it. I love some old gospel stuff. But Christian music…" Her gaze floats around the backyard, searching for the right words. "Christian music isn't really a style of music like rock or the blues. It's really more of a song theme, like love songs."

"So?"

"So listening to it all the time, and nothing else, it's like listening to love songs all the time and nothing else."

"So? Would that be so horrible?"

"Yes. Because nobody's in love all the time."

"So? Maybe we *would* be in love all the time if we listened to love songs all the time."

LeighAnn laughs and shakes her head at the same time. "Just so you know, I hated girls like you when I was in high school."

"Girls like me how?"

"The smiley, sunny Jesus dorks who think that if anything's wrong in your life, it's because you aren't praying hard enough."

"I don't think that."

"Who think life is clear-cut, and if you say it's not, they decide you're just on drugs or a sinner."

"I do *not* think that! LeighAnn, my best friend drowned and turned into a river ghost. I watched her kill her pa-paw;

she almost killed me. You seriously expect me to tell you life is clear-cut?"

"Yeah, well...maybe you're not that bad. But you can still be pretty obnoxious."

"Naw, you like me despite yourself. Admit it."

"I like you despite *your*self."

We both chuckle, then fall quiet. I slide my fingers up and down the guitar strings. It sounds like some creature yawning and stretching itself awake. LeighAnn says, "I got kicked out of church for having blue hair."

"Really?"

"Yeah. I'd just broken up with this guy...okay, he cheated on me, and I told him I was ready to forgive him, then he dumped me."

"Ouch. Sorry."

"Definitely not my best moment. But anyway, I was angry and, I don't know, I wanted to be different. So I dyed my hair blue. Then at church, Deacon Andrews—jackass—pulled me aside and said I couldn't come back until it was a normal color. That just made me even madder, so I just never went back." She grabs a stick and throws it for Cookie. I get the feeling she's waiting for me to say something. She's daring me to say anything.

I want to tell LeighAnn God loves her. That He will leave His flock of ninety-nine sheep to search for the one that has gone astray. When it's found, He'll rejoice more of that sheep than the ninety-nine. I want to tell her that more than anything, but I don't know if I believe that anymore, Holly.

"That wasn't right of them," I say, and at least I know it's the truth. "They shouldn't have treated you like that."

"Thanks."

"So . . . what's your favorite gospel song?"

LeighAnn shrugs, flicking her cigarette butt into the yard. "'Uncloudy Day' is good. 'Down by the Riverside.' My mom loves Dolly Parton, so 'Coat of Many Colors' was, like, the first song I ever learned to sing."

She's grinning now. I ask, "Think you can teach me one?"

LeighAnn lights another cigarette, letting it bob in the corner of her mouth. She strums the first few chords of "Down by the Riverside," correcting herself, making sure she's got it right in her head. Then she says, "All right, so you already know the G chord, so you start off with that. Then D seven, then back to G, then a regular D chord. See how it's different from D seven? You have to move all your fingers, but see how that D is the only note that changes in the chord?"

Just then, Tyler raps on the sliding glass door and motions for LeighAnn. She hands the guitar back to me. "Back to practice," she says with a tired sigh.

Alone again, I try to play the new tune. My fingertips start bleeding again, and my knuckles have started to swell. But even though the song is slow and unsteady and full of leaden notes, if I listen close, I can just sense the mojo underneath.

Sixteen

I sleep with my hand wrapped in a hot towel. It's supposed to ease some of the stiffness, but the aching still wakes me up several times during the night. It doesn't help that bruises still cover my arm from where you touched me, Holly.

Dawn breaks. After Stratofortress leaves for work, me and Tyler return to the river, waiting for you. Standing inside our circle of chalk and lime, I stuff my hands into my pockets without thinking, then yelp as another blister tears. My finger starts bleeding and oozing clear liquid. I want to wash it off in the lake, but I'm afraid. I can imagine a soft clay hand grabbing my wrist while I do. Instead, I rinse it with a little water from the bottle I brought. I let it bleed on my shirt and keep watch while Tyler plays "The Drowned Forest."

He plays the same song, over and over. Sometimes I pray, too, the words scattered through the brambles by the wind. There's still no swallows, and I don't see the plants growing like before.

We have to get to the Bandito Burrito early, for a sound check before the gig, so after a while Tyler says, "We might as well go. I don't think she's coming today."

We leave, but we'll be back tomorrow, Holly. We aren't giving up. Please, please, you can't give up on us either.

Tyler is nervous about the show, even though he won't say it. When we get back to Stratofortress's house, Against the Dawn's CD, *Rooster*, is playing so loud I can hear it before stepping through the front gate. Tyler, Max, and Ultimate Steve are loading gear into the Florence Utilities van. LeighAnn pulls me into the bathroom for my first haircut in weeks.

Sitting on the edge of the tub with a towel around my neck, I say, "Make them wispy, not, like, raggedy-looking."

"Don't worry." LeighAnn's cigarette flares in one corner of her mouth; smoke jets out her nostrils. She snips at my bangs, hair falling to the pink tile. "This is going to look great. Wispy bangs look so good with a rectangular face like yours."

"I just don't want people to think I'm deranged or anything. I mean, it's bad enough I've worn the same shirt for three days."

"Are you kidding?" LeighAnn snorts. "Going to a show in clothes you've worn for days? That's rock 'n' roll. You're just a poser until you've crashed on at least a few couches and smell like an old lady's foot."

"I don't smell like—"

"Shh . . . don't move." LeighAnn makes a few more snips, then pulls the towel off my shoulders. "Okay, have a look."

I look in the mirror. Behind me, LeighAnn purses her lips. "Maybe we should thin them out a tiny—"

"No, they're perfect. Just like they are. Perfect." They really are, longish and side-swept.

"Ahhh!" Grabbing my shoulders, LeighAnn shakes me hard. "Your first real rock show! Are you excited?"

"Yes, yes." I wiggle out of her grip. Part of me is excited, practically straining through my skin to jump around and be loud. Another part of me feels guilty about the first part—enjoying myself while you're still lost under the water. But I think it's important to support Stratofortress after they've helped me so much.

Brushing stray hairs off my shoulders, LeighAnn says, "Now, all through the show, you've just got to be on top of it. Holler, bang on the table, flop around a little. Make it like every song we play is better than sex in a Mustang."

"Gross."

"Or holding a bake sale or reading to blind orphans, whatever. But you have to show the rest of the audience how great the band is. If the cute girl thinks they're great, everybody else will, too."

"Got it."

With all the equipment in the van, there's barely any room left for people. I ride sitting on top of an amp. With the window slid open, I can feel the cool dry air on my face. I can taste the pine trees on the wind. Night presses downtown, squeezing every light into a diamond.

The Bandito Burrito stands in that crummy shopping center near UNA. Greasy yellow light oozes across the parking lot, and the air inside smells like burnt flour, but some college kids survive on their two-dollar vegetarian burritos and nightly gumbo of music acts.

"Jessie! Hey!"

On the little stage, Against the Dawn gobbles enchiladas while doing their sound check. Jessie wears green plaid board shorts and a black T-shirt. Hopping down to give LeighAnn a hug, she says, "Hey, guys. Thanks for coming through for us."

"No problem. How's the tour so far?"

"Pretty good. Birmingham was hell, but other than that, pretty good."

"This is Tyler, our new rhythm guitar. And this is Jane. She ran away from Sesame Street and lives with us now."

"O … kay. Hey."

"Hi," I say.

"So, I'm getting a drink," LeighAnn says. "But you're still staying with us, right?"

"Yes. You don't know what I'd do for a shower right now."

I follow LeighAnn to the bar, where she spots somebody else she knows. "Landon, you made it! All right, man." She hugs a curly haired guy with John Lennon glasses. The girl he's with scowls, but LeighAnn doesn't notice or doesn't care.

Landon says, "Thanks for emailing me. I couldn't believe it when you said Jessie already has an album out and everything."

"I know. Isn't it awesome?" LeighAnn turns to the waitress and says, "Give me a Naked Pig and Mountain Dew for her." While she's catching up with Landon, the waitress opens a bottle of Naked Pig Pale Ale for her, then hands me a fizzing Mountain Dew.

"So what are you up to?" Landon asks.

"Uh . . . still at the bank." When she says it, LeighAnn glances everywhere except into Landon's eyes. You can tell she hates saying that.

"Oh. Well, how's the band? What is it, Secret Fortress?"

"Stratofortress."

"Right, right. Well, how's it going?"

"Okay. We lost our rhythm guitar. We've just got a fill-in for tonight."

"Oh. Where'd Patterson go?"

They talk for a while, then spot more people they know. I see Britney standing by herself and drift over to her. "Hey."

"Hey." She gives me a hug. "So you excited?"

"Yeah. Crowd isn't very big, though."

"It's okay for a Thursday gig." Britney shrugs, surveying the twenty or so people lumped around tables. Most of them are probably just here to eat and really don't care about the band. But Max explained it to me earlier. Against the Dawn is paying for this tour out of their own pockets, so they can't afford to lie around hotel rooms in between big weekend shows. All week, they've been playing in little restaurants and coffee shops, scrambling to get enough gas money to make it to St. Louis tomorrow for the LouFest music festival.

Me and Britney find a table near the stage. The waitress comes by, and Britney orders the sweet potato burrito; I nurse my Mountain Dew. We both cheer as Max adjusts the microphone.

"Um, hey. We're Stratofortress." The mike turns his voice into a hollow rasp. A blue piece of paper crinkles in his hand. "So, um, before I get started, the management asked me to tell you that, in accordance with the Alabama Clean Indoor Air Act, smoking is banned in all indoor workplaces including bars and restaurants, excluding designated hotel and motel smoking rooms and limousines under private hire…" While going over the necessary signage for designated outdoor smoking areas, Max shakes a Winston out of a half-empty pack and lights up. "…Shall assess a civil penalty not to exceed fifty dollars for the first violation, not to exceed one hundred dollars for the second violation, and not to exceed two hundred dollars for each subsequent violation." Stuffing the paper into his shirt pocket and swinging his guitar up, he blows a gray curl of smoke into the stage lights. "But, you know, I won't tell if you don't."

That gets a few laughs from the guys beside the wall. Then Max starts belting the lyrics for "Molotov in Your Pocket" with just Ultimate's drums behind him. Then all three guitars come in at the same moment, and purple veins bulge from the sides of Max's neck. His body jerks hard, side to side. This isn't the Max I've been staying with. It's not even the Max I've watched fuss over songs in practice. This beast couldn't practice a song any more than I could practice crying or laughing.

Tyler misses a chord. He recovers quickly, though, and if I hadn't heard the song a million times, I probably wouldn't have noticed. Then he misses the same chord again, and this time, LeighAnn glances over, annoyed. When the song ends, she walks over and talks to Tyler. I can't hear what she's saying, but Tyler nods. Downstage, Max pants into the mike and says, "Okay, this, um, this one was inspired by Dr. Phil. I was watching his show once, and he said, 'Cheers to a new year and another chance to get it right,' and I thought that was too good a line for Dr. Phil to have, so I stole it."

They start playing "Cheers." Before long, the momentum of the song sweeps me along and I stop worrying. As I open my mouth to holler, Tyler messes up again. Then he stops dead, and the other instruments clatter to a stop after him.

Feedback whines as Stratofortress glances at each other, trying to get on cue. "If it was perfect, it wouldn't be rock 'n' roll," Max chuckles as they start up again. But Tyler has that deer-in-headlights look now, and his right hand is stiff against the strings. He loses the song again, and boos rise from the crowd. The table beside the wall starts chanting, "You suck! You suck! You suck!"

This time, Max sets down his guitar and walks offstage. He comes straight for us, and at first I think he's coming to yell at me. Instead, he grabs Britney's beer and drinks. "It's not that bad," she says weakly, almost drowned out by the chanting.

Max doesn't answer. He goes back on stage, not looking at Tyler, and when he steps to the microphone, he sounds like nothing's wrong, like he's having the time of his life. "Okay, thanks for having us. We've got one more for you. This is 'Catatonic State Marching Band.'"

I wonder why they're giving up on "Cheers" halfway through, but then I see. They play "Catatonic State" so simple and fast, it would be hard for anybody to notice if Tyler did mess up. He could stop playing altogether and people would barely hear it under Steve's exploding drums. Still, the "You suck" chant keeps going, underneath the song.

It's a couple college boys behind us. I turn around and

glare at them, and I hate them. I want to throw my drink in their faces. I want to smash the glass against their heads. I know it's not right, but it would feel so good to hear their smug, stupid chant shatter into shrieks. It would feel good to watch them skitter backward like crabs.

Then a gray-goateed man comes up—he wears a greasy apron across his huge belly. He slaps one bear-paw of a hand on the college boys' table, says one word, and they shut up. But they're still snickering, and I still hate them.

Stratofortress makes it to the end of the song, Max tells people to stick around for Against the Dawn, and they get out of there. Me and Britney cheer as they walk offstage, but everybody else ignores them.

When Steve comes to our table, Britney says, "That was . . . you recovered really—"

Steve shakes his head. "Baby, leave it alone."

"Well, I mean, with 'Catatonic State,' I think you really got back—"

"Just leave it alone, okay?" he snaps. Then he hugs her and sighs. "Come on, let's go sit with Max and LeighAnn."

I glance back and see them sitting at the shadowy back of the room, already drinking. "Can't they come up here?"

"No. I don't want to be up front right now."

While we move to the back table, Tyler motions to me from near the stage. He has his guitar case in his hand. "I'm gonna go. Do you need anything out of my truck?"

"What? No. Come watch Against the Dawn with us."

"No, I messed up. I . . ." He looks ready to cry. "I'm gonna go. I'll talk to you tomorrow, okay?"

"What? Where you gonna go? Your truck's back at Strato-fortress's house."

"I'll just walk. I have to get out of here."

"No. Tyler, please. Come watch Against the Dawn with us."

"No, I messed up. I ... they don't want me, right now."

"Tyler ... "

"I'll see you tomorrow." And he's gone.

I go sit with Stratofortress. For a long time, nobody says anything. Nobody looks at each other or around at the crowd that saw them bomb. They all stare at their drinks or hands or the table.

"Well ... " Max mutters. "Nobody burst into flame while onstage. If you look at it that way, it was a success."

We snort and chuckle. Steve says, "I don't know. Halfway through, I was sort of hoping to burst into flame."

We laugh out loud. LeighAnn hugs Max. Stratofortress is still embarrassed, still angry, but at least they can lift their heads up now. I try a bite of Britney's sweet potato burrito. It's just as vile as it sounds.

Then the music crashes down like a wave. No intro. No warning. Against the Dawn jumps into "Boomtown" with both feet, then "In a Brown Beat Coat." Stratofortress didn't do much to excite the crowd, but Against the Dawn makes up for it, barreling through one song after another with barely a breath in between. Then Jessie stops to tell a long story about not being allowed to drink Cokes growing up because she was Mormon. Except one day, she snuck into the woods with a neighbor boy to trade peeks at her underwear for a can of Coke.

"Tony left me. He went on home, but I was too ashamed. I stayed in the woods, those tall pines all around, that sweet taste still in my mouth." She cracks open another beer, drinks deep, and wipes the foam off her chin. "I cried. Just sat on this old tree trunk and sobbed and prayed to God to forgive me while it got darker and colder. But even while I was praying, there was part of me that just wanted another Coke. And I knew I was a bad girl and I was going to Hell."

Tugging her guitar strap down so her bass shifts onto her back, Jessie starts singing, "Oh darling, oh darling, don't tell me no lie. Where did you sleep last night?" Staring up at the lights, she answers her own question—a one-girl call-and-response. "I slept in the pines where the sun never shines and shivered when the cold wind blowed."

Only the guitarist accompanies her as she moans, "You've slighted me once, you've slighted me twice. You'll never slight me no more... You've caused me to weep, you've caused me to mourn, you've caused me to leave my home..."

The song creeps up my spine like frost. It makes me think of you, Holly, lost in the drowned forest. But just before I crumple under the sadness of the strange tune, Jessie lets out a triumphant whoop and launches into "Over the Wall." The band plays so loud behind her, I half expect Jessie to whirl offstage like a dead leaf.

I recognize the songs from their CD, but music is different live. I can taste the steel strings in the air. Some people crowd around the stage and I join them, stomping my feet against the floor until it hurts. I enjoy the hurt. I start pogoing up and down. I can't help it. My heart pounds in my chest, keeping time with the song.

A guy starts dancing with me, grinning wide. He's slim and hard, arms and hips just brushing mine. When the song ends, he leans close. "Hey, what's up? I'm Jello."

"Jello?" I giggle.

"Uh-huh. So how's it feel being the prettiest girl in the room?"

I laugh out loud at that, and Ultimate Steve and Max appear on either side of me. Ultimate says, "I give up, Jello. How does it feel?"

"The hell's your problem?" Jello bows up his shoulders and jerks his arms toward his chest, swaying in Ultimate's face like a cobra.

Ultimate shrugs. "No problem. Unless you want one."

LeighAnn tugs me back to our corner. "Damn, Sesame Street. Gonna put a leash on you."

"He didn't do anything. We were just having fun."

"Yeah, you and Jello have different ideas about fun. Stick with us, okay?"

"Yeah, yeah."

She wraps an arm around my shoulders. Ultimate and Max come back, and Jello slinks to the bar.

The show leaves a ringing in my ears, almost painful but not quite. Afterward, Against the Dawn hangs around the bar, chatting with people, selling CDs and T-shirts. Stratofortress orders another round. I sip my Mountain Dew and walk around, still too wound up to sit still.

The stage is small, just plywood boards covered in white

scratches. I lie back, staring up at the mic stand and warm lights. I stretch my hands out and feel the stage's hardness and the energy beneath the hardness. The stage holds life inside it, like a mussel shell or a seed.

"Jane, you okay?" LeighAnn leans over me.

I sit up. "Yeah, I just … I love you."

One side of LeighAnn's mouth curls up like a sideways question mark. "Did you have something to drink? Did one of the guys—"

"No. You took me in, and you didn't have to, and maybe didn't even want to, but you treat me like I'm your sister, and you're—I just love you is all." I hug her.

"It's okay. Don't even worry about it." She pats my back. "And you sure you haven't been drinking?"

"No. I mean, yes, I'm sure."

"Good, because someone needs to drive home."

"Huh? Not me. I'm fifteen."

"And we're all drunk." She shrugs. "But we can't leave Against the Dawn's gear in this neighborhood, so you've got to get us and it and everything home."

"I don't have my learner's permit yet."

"It's only a few miles, and there's basically no traffic this late. It'll be easy. Just remember, left pedal goes, right pedal slows." She takes a few steps, then shakes her head. "No, wait. That's backward. Remember it, but remember it backward."

We help Against the Dawn load their gear into the 4Runner that's been their home for a month. The guitarist, Kirk, gives us the grand tour. Two people can sleep stretched out if one of them lies on top of the road cases. The only food is a plastic tub of pretzels—payment from their Birmingham gig.

Ultimate drives the Florence Utilities van home, with Britney beside him looking out for cops. I climb into the 4Runner's driver's seat. LeighAnn, Max, Jessie, and Against the Dawn's drummer—a blonde girl whose name I didn't catch—crowd into the backseat. Kirk sits in the passenger seat. Feeling very small behind the wheel, I roll over the curb while turning out of the parking lot and lurch down the road. Kirk says, "Um. You probably want to turn on your headlights."

"Dang it." I tug on a lever. The windshield wipers come on. "Dang, dang, dang it."

Reaching around me, Kirk turns the wipers off and switches on the headlights. "Relax, you're doing great."

The traffic light turns yellow, and I jam the brakes. Cuss words fly as we're tossed forward.

Jessie says, "Hey, Sesame Street, turn here. I wanna see the Indian mound."

Kirk turns around. "The what?"

Drunk, Jessie struggles with the words. "It's a Mith—Missith—Mississippian mound by Wilson Lake. It's right up here."

I butt in. "Actually, I think I should just get you guys—"

"No, no, I'm curious now," Kirk says. "Come on, Sesame Street."

"It'll be okay, Jane," Max says. "Just keep an eye out for cops, and it'll be okay."

So I turn and cross the train tracks to where the thousand-year-old earthwork heaves up between warehouses and an office complex. There's the semi-circular embankment protecting a grassy field as flat as a cake. Inside lies the steep, hexagonal mound. Once, a mighty warrior was entombed here. He was buried with a club that was embedded with shark teeth and fishhooks made from antler. They dug him up and put him in the museum decades ago, though, so all that's left is the half-forgotten mound. We climb single-file up the steps cut into its clay, up above the streetlights, and look out over the river.

Stratofortress and Against the Dawn stand around drinking beers and telling jokes. They don't talk about how bad Stratofortress's set was, but it doesn't seem like Against the Dawn is mad or anything. Jessie plonks down on the mound's weedy crown, tucking her legs under her. "I used to bike out here after class. Loved it, wrote so many good songs up here. Max! You need to come out here to write your songs."

"All right."

"Dude, seriously!"

"All right!"

I sit down beside Jessie. "Did you write that 'where did you sleep' song up here?"

"Huh? 'In the Pines'? No ... no, no." Her head wags back and forth. "I didn't write that. Nobody knows who wrote that. It's so good, though, isn't it?"

"Yeah. It actually scared me a little."

Jessie laughs at that. Kirk says, "If you want to hear a really good version of 'In the Pines,' go find Leadbelly's cover."

LeighAnn says, "Yeah, Nirvana did a version of it too that's really good."

Max starts singing, and Jessie joins in. "Oh darling, oh

darling, don't tell me no lie. Where did you sleep last night? I slept in the pines where the sun never shines and shivered when the cold wind blowed."

I listen, staring out at the river, dark and shining like knapped flint. The song is even more haunting out here, as the notes mingle with the thick, fetid smell blowing off the water. We know the smell from fishing trips, Holly, from wading thigh-deep through inlets boiling with frogspawn. And for the rest of my life, I'll know it as the smell you carried up from the drowned forest with you. It filled the houseboat's cabin until my eyes watered.

It's the smell of rot. It's fish, leaves, and a million dead things turning to muck. But it's also the smell of life, isn't it, Holly? The river breaks dead things down into humus, into raw life-stuff. Before they built the dam, the river would flood its banks every summer, covering the land with the soft black soil that turns our valley green. It's why the Indians lived along the river and why farmers settled in the holler. It's why the kudzu vines twist their way up power lines and swallow abandoned houses. It grows so thick, you can hardly keep it cut back.

The river takes dead things and coaxes new life from them. It's why the Mississippians buried their beloved here, on the banks of immortality. It's why, every summer at Rivercall, we drown people so they can be reborn into a Christ-centered life. We depend on the water's power to grow new green shoots from old, sin-rotten wood. Maybe that's what gives the river its mojo, Holly. Maybe it's why you didn't quite die when you drowned.

Squealing laughter behind me makes me turn. Drummer Girl is rolling down the mound, followed by LeighAnn. Jessie and Max ignore them and keep singing. "You've slighted me once, you've slighted me twice. You'll never slight me no more..."

———————

"You've caused me to weep, you've caused me to mourn, you've caused me to leave my home..." Pouring water into the coffeemaker, I sing softly and sway my hips.

I gave Drummer Girl the couch last night. She's stretched out, one arm draped over her eyes. Jessie and Kirk lie on the floor. None of them snore. That's probably a huge advantage if you're touring with people.

While the coffee is brewing, I lean my elbows on the rough wood table and clasp my hands together. I've prayed, a couple minutes at least, every day I've been here, even though my mind constantly wanders—like right now. Still, I ask God to comfort my family and to protect Against the Dawn when they head out on the road today. I try to think of things to be thankful for. I try to ignore the part of my brain moaning that God isn't listening.

Done with that chore, I step outside. Even this ragged neighborhood seems beautiful in the wash of cool, early sunlight. I head to Piggly Wiggly, singing the whole way.

Just me and some stock boys in the store. I walk up and down the aisles, getting bologna, bread, sliced cheese, and the biggest head of lettuce they've got. When I step back outside, I have forty-three cents to my name.

Stratofortress and Britney have already shuffled off, red-eyed and hungover, for long days at work. Against the Dawn is still asleep. I make sandwiches, spreading on mayonnaise and mustard from the little packets LeighAnn swipes from restaurants. The lettuce smells good, still faintly like the earth. The bread is soft and supple. It all smells good.

I keep singing, under my breath so I won't wake anyone up. Somewhere, "In the Pines" turns into "Five Loaves and Two Fishes."

An alarm chirps in the living room, and I hear mumbling. Kirk comes into the kitchen. "Hey, Sesame Street, you're already up?"

"Didn't go to bed."

"And now you're making a tower of sandwiches."

"They're for you. For the road."

"Wow, thanks."

"Your clothes are all folded on the table. I don't know what belongs to who, so you'll have to sort it out."

He looks at them, then looks at me. "Sesame Street, you're the best groupie ever."

But they've got a gig in St. Louis tonight and need to get moving. Jessie leaves some band stickers on the table, writing a note to LeighAnn on the back of one. While they take turns in the bathroom, I hurry up with the sandwiches. I run out of bologna, so the last three are peanut butter.

When I carry them out in the Piggly Wiggly sack, the band has almost finished loading the 4Runner. Grinning, Drummer

Girl takes the sandwiches and hugs me. I hug my way down the line. "Bye. Be careful, okay? The show was great last night, and I'm going to tell everybody to buy your—your—"

My voice cracks. Jessie is skinny the way you were skinny, Holly. When I hug her I feel the points of her shoulder blades, the energy humming through her like a live wire. You might have gone on tour like this too, huh? If you'd lived a few more years? Tears blur my vision. I squeeze Jessie tighter.

"You . . . you okay?" she asks.

"Yeah. It's—it's just—" Now? Weeks of not being able to cry, and I start now? This is so stupid. I'm weirding them out. "Just be careful, okay? And you were great. And go kick butt in St. Louis."

"Okay. You sure you're okay?"

"Yeah. I'm fine." But I can't stop crying. My heart is too full, Holly. I have nothing, and all I want to do is give every-thing—hugs, my spot on the couch, sandwiches. I'd give them the forty-three cents if I thought they'd take it. Instead, I wave as the 4Runner turns at the end of the street and disappears.

Alone in the quiet house, I keep crying while sipping steel-wool coffee. I don't have any people left to hug, so I head out back and hug Hobbit and Cookie.

"I love you, Hobbit. Yes, I love you too, Cookie, oh yes, oh yes."

It's strange, Holly. Last night, before the show, I felt guilty about going. I didn't think it was right to enjoy myself while you were still lost. I guess maybe it's the same guilt Jessie felt after drinking that Coke, the shame of being made from weak, craving flesh. But you don't know what it's like when your heart's numb, when you can't laugh or cry. Carrying that useless lump around in my chest felt a lot more like Hell, like being cast into the outer darkness, than any sin ever has.

Last night, I danced, Holly. I yelled, I sang, I felt my heart beating for the first time in a long time. That's what I give thanks for today, Holly—my heart isn't broken all the way. It's still beating, even when it beats out an aching melody like "In the Pines."

Seventeen

Stratofortress's house is empty, and I'm back to practicing "Mary Had a Little Lamb." A car passes by trailing rap music. A bottle rocket left over from Fourth of July whistles into the sky and explodes.

It's afternoon when Tyler shows up. I step out on the porch to meet him, and we head to Swallow's Nest Bluff.

"So, have they said anything?" Tyler asks once we're on the road.

"Not really. I don't think... it really wasn't that bad, you know?" Except it was. Those seconds of silence when he just stopped playing, they seemed to stretch forever.

"They shouldn't have asked me to play with them. I shouldn't have said yes. I let them down. I..." Tyler shakes his head and doesn't say anything else. At the bluff, we clamber down the slope and draw our protective circle through the tough wild grass. We play music for you and watch the water lap at the stones.

Tyler plays the "The Drowned Forest" over and over, flawlessly, then "Down by the Riverside." When he stops for a sip of water, I ask, "So why can you play great here, but not last night?"

"Don't know. I just—I don't know. I made one mistake, then another, and then I was panicking and just kept making mistakes."

"Well, it was your first time playing a real gig. It's not surprising you got nervous."

"Yeah." He fidgets with the water-bottle cap. "I thought it'd be like church, but I know everybody at church. I don't have to win them over, you know?"

"Sure."

"Same thing with the Banana Hammocks. We mostly just played for friends, mostly just goofed around. Last night was the first gig that really, really mattered, and I blew it. I totally froze up."

I nod. "Still, I wish you'd stayed last night. It was the most fun I've had in a long time, since Holly died."

"Against the Dawn's a great band. I just—"

"No. I mean, it was the most alive I've felt. And I wish you'd felt it too."

Tyler chuckles and nudges me with his shoulder. "I'm alive. Trust me, I know." He starts playing again, but I put my hand on the strings to silence them.

"It also made me realize death can't stop life. Death ends one life, but it just starts another."

"What?"

I'm not explaining it right. It all seemed crystal clear

sitting on the Indian mound. "It's just, we're going to put Holly to rest sooner or later. And then we're going to move on, you know? We're going to have to figure out new lives without her. That's scary to think about."

"So, what? You think I messed up last night on purpose so I wouldn't have to move on? Like, I sabotaged myself because I'm scared?"

"No. But being scared makes it easier to run away after you screwed up. It makes it easy to just curl up inside old memories. It's the same as not coming to church now. Or not joining the praise band when Bo asked you."

"Quit! You don't know what you're talking about. Just watch the water, okay?"

"Yes, I do know what I'm talking about. I know because I feel it too. It's scary. Holly's been my best friend since forever. I don't even know who I am without her. And when this is over, I'm going to have to let go of her, and that's scary, Tyler."

"Just watch, Jane." He starts to play.

"No. I want to talk." But Tyler ignores me and keeps playing. I cross my arms and watch the water as evening settles around us like ash. A tear stings the corner of my eye. Too mad to let Tyler see me cry, I wipe it away quickly. For the millionth time, I wish you were here, Holly. Not your ghost, but really you. I wish you could tell us how you survived after your parents' death, how you found the courage to build a new life all on your own.

Except you weren't all on your own, were you?

"Tyler, stop. Stop! Holly's not coming. She's not here."

"What?"

I rap my knuckles against my head, hard enough to hurt. "Think about it. Auntie Peake said Holly was just lost. But she was lost before—I mean, she must have felt lost when her parents died—and *that* time, her grandparents took her in."

Tyler puts his hand to his mouth. "So she'd go looking for them this time, too. She's not coming out of the river because she's already gone home."

Eighteen

I sit on a toolbox in the back of the van, craning around Max's headrest. Tyler's in the front seat, giving directions. "Turn here. Foster Mill Road."

When Max turns, Ultimate looks at me. "You know this is breaking and entering, right? If you get arrested, saying you thought your dead friend might have gone home isn't going to help much."

"Who'll call the police? Who worries if there's a utility van parked in front of an empty house? Just act like you're fixing the power or whatever, and nobody'll notice us. Turn left up here."

Catching my eye in the rearview mirror, Max says, "You're giving off a real sneaky, criminal-mastermindy vibe. You know that?"

He means it as a sly compliment, I know. But I can't summon a laugh or even a smile. "This house here. With the blue trim."

Your house, without love, the porch steps lost in a fog of

Queen Anne's lace. Your house with a living room window broken. Your house surrounded by swallows. The birds that left their nests on the bluff—they're all here, slashing between the orange sky and shadowed tree branches.

Max steers into the driveway. "So what do we do now?"

"Go look."

LeighAnn says, "Jane, you shouldn't rush … "

I hop out as soon as the van stops. The driveway of white pebbles has melted like a snowbank, green grass nibbling at its edges. The swallows have built mud nests under the porch eaves. They build their homes from the same mud and sticks you build your body from. They saw you drown, saw you reshape yourself, and somehow they consider you kin. They love you and followed you here.

Ultimate, carrying his toolbox, pretends to check the meter. The others follow me up to the porch. Birds wheel up and out, dive straight down screaming at us. They saw you drown. Maybe, if they love you, they hate me and Tyler for not saving you. I hunch forward, ignoring them, and climb the steps.

The door handle has rusted away. I can see where you tugged on it until it finally crumbled in your hand. The pieces still lie on the porch. You cried for somebody to let you in, banged and scratched on the door until the panel rotted, knots in the painted pine sprouting stubby new branches.

I nudge the door open. "Holly?"

Tyler follows close behind, holding the bag of chalk and lime. He clicks on a flashlight and swings it around, into the corners.

"Holly? It's Jane."

The air inside is humid and still, heavy with the fecund stink of the lake bottom. Stalks of goldenseal grow from the carpet, hairy-stemmed and scarlet-berried. Even this far from the river, you carry its powers of rot and wild growth.

Max and LeighAnn watch from just inside the doorway. "Jane ... this isn't a great—"

I wave at LeighAnn to shut up, then call down the hall, "Holly? It's Jane. Don't be scared, okay? Okay?"

No answer. A few wrinkled snapshots lie at the mouth of the hall. I kneel down, flip one over. Water damage has blurred the colors and figures, but it's a picture of some band onstage. It's one of the photos from your pa-paw's houseboat. I remember the photo we found of your me-maw. The wind didn't blow it onto the shore; you dropped it.

Tyler yells, "Oh, God!"

I rush over and shoulder past him, pushing into the kitchen while he backpedals out. "Holly, it's me! It's Jane! I've been look—"

"Jane. Look at it, Jane." Tyler takes my elbow. I blink and look again, seeing what's in front of me. Shaped from mud and flotsam, the miserable copy of you lies stiff, dried out, and crumbling on the tile. Whatever scrap of your soul held it together has unraveled. Another copy crouches near the pantry, knees pulled up, face buried in earthen arms. As it dried out, one shoulder split away from the body. Ants crawl out of the wound.

"So ... how are there two of them? Two of her, or whatever?" LeighAnn asks.

"She can reshape herself over and over." Tyler glances from one body to the other. "She came once, but that body broke apart. So she formed a second body and came again. The heat. She must have come at night when it's cool, but during the day, when it gets hot, the mud dries out and falls apart."

"Why'd she come back at all?" Max asks. "There's nothing here. What's she looking for?"

"She's looking for her grandparents," I say.

Wings flutter inside the house. I look down the hall to see the cobalt bird dart into your bedroom. I follow it, knowing I don't want to see.

One body is curled up on the bed, the sheets growing mossy beneath it and kudzu vines twisting around the rust-brown bed frame. Other husks crouch in the corners or have just dropped to their knees. One has gray teeth made from pieces of mussel shell. I try counting the bodies, but they've crumbled together—hands broken off spindly arms, chests crushed underfoot. There's more trash carried up from the houseboat, too—a clock radio is plugged in but not working, more ruined pictures are propped carefully against the baseboards. Moldering clothes have been folded and stacked. They've started sprouting mushrooms from your touch. You even carried up your pa-paw's guitar. You lie with fingers still encrusted around the Dreadnought's neck.

I cover my mouth and try to look away, but there's nowhere to look where you aren't. Swooping to the jagged lip of the broken window, the swallow chitters, laughing at me for coming here, then vanishes outside.

LeighAnn says, "Listen, if Holly comes at night, we need to get out of here."

How many times have you made your way home, Holly? Do you even remember, from one night to the next? Or do you walk all the way here, think you've finally made it, then find a room full of your crumbling selves?

"Jane? We need to go, Jane."

I shake my head. "I can't let her just keep coming here and coming here. I have to stay and say Auntie Peake's prayer over her."

"Last time you tried to help her, she almost killed you," LeighAnn says.

"If you want to go, go." I shake my head. "I'm not asking anybody to stay."

"If anyone stays, it'll be safer for everybody to stay," Max says.

"Safer for who?" LeighAnn snaps. "You just want to see her for yourself."

"Well, sorta, but come on, Lee-Lee. We can't just leave them here."

"I can't believe this. This is crazy. I can't believe this." LeighAnn cradles her stomach like she's ready to puke. Then she sighs. "So what do we do until she shows up?"

Nineteen

Your neighbors call their kids in from playing. TVs flicker blue inside living rooms for a while, then windows go dark one by one. The Bradford pear tree in your backyard blooms pale white in the moonlight. Can't you remember building bed-sheet tents against the tree's trunk, Holly? Pressed together in the tight secret space, we told stories and imagined what we would do when we grew up. The shadows below the branches were jeweled with sunlight.

I turn away and watch the street. Stratofortress watches too, LeighAnn blowing whorls of cigarette smoke against the grimy rear window of the van. Every noise makes them whip around, but nobody's said a word in an hour.

After a while, the silence seems to press down on us. Tyler clear his throat and mumbles, "Hey, guys? I just ... you know ... sorry. About the other night."

Max nods. "It's okay. I mean, we know you have a lot to worry about right now. It's just that the UNA students, they're our main audience right now. Those guys who saw the show are going to talk, and, well, you kind of screwed us."

Tyler tugs at his hair. "Yeah. I get that. I'm sorry."

I glance at Ultimate—Tyler's biggest supporter in the band—hoping he'll say something. Instead, he just claps Tyler on the back.

"So, have you thought about a permanent replacement?" Tyler asks, trying to put on a brave face.

"Uh, let's not worry about that right now." Max shakes his head. "I mean—"

"Guys, quiet," LeighAnn hisses. "Listen to the birds."

The swallows have started crying in the dark, all at once. While the crescendo rises, Max asks, "What? What's happening?"

"I don't know. Quiet. Just keep—"

Only a silhouette, pushing through the bushes, but I recognize the way you walk and your slender, winter-tree shape. You're a beanpole, Holly. You take after your pa-paw. Somehow, when you were alive, I never noticed how delicate you were. When you disappear into the house, I slip out of the van. There's a horrible feeling in my stomach, like my intestines are being teased out through my belly button. This will kill you all over again. I'll have to watch all over again. But I keep creeping forward.

Behind me, Stratofortress squawks worse than the swallows, but this is just you and me, wrapped inside the night as warm as those years-ago bed-sheet tents. Can't you remember musty sleeping bags and flashlight beams playing against the fabric walls? Remember talking, talking, talking for hours until we fell asleep—your hand in mine? Didn't you know then that I'd never, ever abandon you?

In the living room, curtained windows leave blades of pale light on the carpet. From the kitchen archway, I see spiky growths sprouting along your spine like potato eyes. I'm glad it's so dark in here.

"Pa-paw? Pa-paw, where are you?" You notice one of the husks on the floor—one of your old selves. Standing motionless and staring, arms dangling at your sides, you try to understand. My urge is to reach out and comfort you. Luckily, Tyler takes my elbow and silently pulls me away from the archway. He punctures the bag of chalk and lime with his thumb, drawing a circle around us in ghost-white powder. I watch, trying not to hear you whimpering as you see the other bodies, too.

A swallow lands on the windowsill. Another drops, chittering, into my hair. I wave it away, then from the kitchen I hear, "Jane? Jane, is that you?"

The bird flutters around me, then joins its friend on the sill. They talk in their excited language. They're telling you I'm here.

You come around the corner, voice oozing. "Pa-paw's gone, Jane. I think something bad has happened."

"Get back! Don't!" I yell.

But the magic circle works. Your whine sharpens to an iron-nail shriek when you try to cross.

"Wha...? Jane! Tyler?"

"It's going to be okay, Holly. We're going—no, don't come—"

Your scream pierces my chest. When you drop to hands

and knees, my arms ache to reach out. Auntie Peake's magic hurts me as much as it does you.

"It's okay, Holly. We're going to help, okay? But we have to pray. Lord, guide this troubled soul—Holly, pray with me—soul to rest. Carry her from darkness—"

"Jane, I need help."

"—from darkness and cold evermore, for those washed clean in Your—"

"Jane!" Wildflowers boil up from the carpet around your knees. They curve around the circle but can't enter.

"—washed clean in Your blood shall fear not. Amen."

"Everybody's gone. Help me find Pa-paw, okay? Please?"

Why won't you die? Please, just die.

I clasp my hands so tightly they shake. "Lord, guide this troubled soul to rest. Carry her from darkness and cold evermore, for those washed clean in Your blood shall fear not. Amen." But the prayer is worthless babble. Our Lord has cast us out and shown us His back. I don't know why. I'm so sorry, Holly.

"Holly, stop!"

You stretch your arm out toward me, then yank it back, screaming. You can't reach past the circle. The chalk and lime burns you somehow. Still, you reach for me again. The circle holds. Your mouth widens in a miserable howl, widens so much your cheek splits open. The beetles wiggling out look like fat black teardrops.

"It's okay, Holly. I'm here. I—" I reach past the line of chalk and lime. Somewhere beyond you and me, Tyler shouts, but I can't stop myself.

Joining with mine, your fingers are slick but strong. Tissues of clay and dead weeds tighten, drawing the heat from my skin.

"I'd never leave you, Holly. You know."

"Help ... help, please."

I want to tell you I will, but the words catch in my throat as the coldness of the river seeps up my arm. Fingers dig into my wrist. Roots sprout from my palm, tangling my flesh to yours.

I can feel the river's mojo, Holly. I can feel its deep, cool anger. You drowned but refused to die. You wouldn't let the river break you down into raw life-stuff. So it breaks down whatever you touch—the tighter you hold on, the faster it slips away. The river keeps the living world always just out of your reach.

I don't want to die, Holly. Gasp, pull, kick; the tendrils creep toward my heart.

"No, Jane! Jane, we have to find Pa—"

Thuck! The blur of motion twists your head around. Max brings the wrench down again. *Thuck!*

Tyler pulls me back. Pain burns sparkler-hot down my arm and hand and fingers—the roots ripping free. He drags me toward the door. I try to get free, but he won't let me go. Craning my head around, I see Max grab you, shove you into the magic circle.

"Jane ... " You crawl forward, then cringe back from the line of chalk and lime, now trapped inside the circle. "Jane?" Max's work boot stomps a deep hole in your side.

I look away. I'm sorry, Holly. Tyler rushes me back out under the starless sky.

In the van, the city lights sweep through the windows and across LeighAnn's expression. My rotting shirt tears like paper in her hands as she checks me all over. The tendrils and roots disgust her. While plucking them from my skin, her face turns as pale as the moon. "Why didn't you stay in the circle?" she asks, almost pleading. "You were—"

"LeighAnn? Lee-Lee?" Max sits among loose tools and spools of wire. He pants hard, trying to keep panic down. White blisters on the palms of his hands burst open with bloody dandelion heads.

She scrambles to him. He grits he teeth when she pulls one out, and I remember him grabbing you, Holly, pushing you away from me.

"Why did you reach out of the circle?" LeighAnn shrieks at me. "You were safe. We were all—how was that too damn hard for you?" Steam spent, she turns, cradles Max's head, and teases the flowers out as quickly as she can with trembling fingers.

I tear plants from my skin, accepting the pain that makes my hands shake, letting the blood drip off my elbows. Bile splashes the back of my throat, but I refuse to make a sound.

Twenty

My hand is swollen and purple like strange fruit. The scabs keep breaking, oozing blood that stains my shorts. Tyler spent the night here, tossing on the living room floor. Even though he couldn't really do anything, he wanted to stay close by. At least it's Saturday, so none of Stratofortress have to go to work. Ultimate went to Britney's, though, and LeighAnn and Max have been in their bedroom all morning. When I hear Max crying, I go to see if he's okay. Before I can ask, though, LeighAnn pushes me back out into the hall.

"Getting dangerous keeping you around, Sesame Street," she says.

"I'm sorry."

LeighAnn studies me.

"Sorry," I say again, quieter. She won't kick me out, but LeighAnn isn't my friend right now, either. The man she loves almost died because I'm an idiot. She gets two cans of Mountain Dew, a box of tissues from the bathroom, and disappears into their bedroom again.

Why didn't I stay in the circle? What did I think I could do?

I go nudge Tyler with my foot. "Hey, wake up."

He jerks up with a gasp, looking all around. "Wh—what is it?"

"We have to talk to Auntie Peake. Figure out why the prayer didn't work."

The drive out to Decatur stretches by in dead silence. We go to Morningside Nursing Home and find Auntie Peake sitting up in bed like last time. I tell her what happened, but she just shakes her head sadly. "The prayer would have worked for any lost lamb of Christ."

"Well … it didn't."

"Then maybe your friend, maybe in her heart, wasn't as Godly as you think." Auntie Peake won't look at us while she says it.

"No, no. Holly was the best person. She loved God even after He took away her parents."

"Isn't there something else we could try?" Tyler asks. "Another prayer?"

"Any prayer's power comes from faith. Faith in the Lord and love for Him. If your friend didn't have that, no amount of praying will help her. I'm sorry."

I tell her all the good things you did, Holly, how wonderful you were. I tell her how you wrote *FEAR NOT* across your guitar. Auntie Peake just shakes her head. "It doesn't matter if she was a nice person, it only matters if she believed in the power of the Lord. Faith can move mountains and wash the most sinful soul clean. But if your friend doesn't have it, down at the very bottom of her heart, then there's nothing we can do to save her. I'm sorry."

"No!" I shout. "You didn't know her! You don't know what you're talking about!" Then one of the staff comes in and says we have to leave. Now.

I stomp out to the truck. On the road, I keep shouting. "Where does she get off thinking she knows Holly?"

"I don't know," Tyler answers softly.

"She won't help us anymore because she doesn't think Holly had faith? You know what it is? The old bat's probably just embarrassed because her stupid magic didn't work, and now she's trying to blame it on Holly, blame anybody but herself."

Tyler nods. "Maybe. Maybe if we find another root-worker, they can help us."

"Stupid old bat. But … " I pick at a scab, and my anger fades. When it fades, I'm left with doubt, with a question mark like a rusty fishhook. "But what if she's right? What if Holly didn't have any faith left?"

"Of course she did. You just yelled at an old lady for five minutes about how Holly played music at church, had *FEAR NOT* on her guitar."

"I know she said she did, I know she acted like she did, but … what if, down at the bottom of her heart, Holly really didn't love God anymore? What if it was all an act?"

"Why would she act like that, then?"

"I don't know, I don't know. It's just, for weeks now, I've

been trying to figure out how Holly loved God after all she'd been through. And maybe the answer is, she didn't. I mean, we've been through a fraction of what she went through, and you don't love Him anymore, right? I don't love Him." It's the first time I've admitted it out loud, said it to anybody but you, Holly. I start to choke up and struggle to voice the rest of my thought. "What if she didn't have any faith, and that means we can't help her? What if she's just going to be trapped in the drowned forest forever?"

"Hey, hey, no, no. We're gonna find another root-worker, okay? We're going to figure this out, okay? Okay?"

I don't answer. Tyler keeps promising it'll be okay, but he doesn't believe it. He just wants me to stop crying. Hot tears spill down my cheeks as fast as I can wipe them away. I turn my face to the window and watch the trees pass. The pines along Highway 31 rise as straight and narrow as the path to Heaven.

Tyler says, "What about your professor that interviewed all those people? Maybe we can find the rest of his transcripts."

"Frazier? Yeah, maybe."

"Or … we could go back to Holly's house."

That makes me turn back to face him. "What? No way. What for?"

He shrugs. "Maybe we'll see something we didn't see last night."

"And maybe Holly's still there. Or else her neighbors see us and call the police. What do you think is there?"

"I don't know. But I'm not quitting on Holly yet. Maybe Auntie Peake's right and there isn't anything we can do, but

I'm not gonna just take her word for it and give up. I've got a whole list of bad ideas to try before I give up."

That makes me snicker, less because it's actually funny and more because I have to laugh at something.

Tyler says, "I'll drop you off if you—"

"No, I'm in."

"You sure?"

"Positive." I wipe my eyes on my sleeve and pull myself together.

"It's past lunchtime," Tyler says. "Maybe if you had some food in you, you'd feel—"

"No. If we're going to do this, we do it now."

We head back to your house.

Tyler drives past it and around the block before pulling into the driveway. No police or anything. The front door stands wide open now, but the neighbors will ignore it— everyone hoping somebody else will handle it.

The swallows chatter in the pear tree, watching us pass. I throw stones into the branches to drive them away. Inside, the muggy heat sticks to my skin. "Holly?"

You still lie trapped inside the magic circle in the living room. Max's work boot left a sharp imprint in the muddy flesh.

"Holly?"

The mud-pie thing has dried up and died. A wide crack in its chest is full of blood-red sunlight. You've tried to come back to your old life so many times, but the drowned forest keeps gobbling you back down. You'll come tonight too, won't you, Holly? You'll try to resist the river's mojo, but it will win, over and over and over, and there's nothing I can do to stop you or save you. The drowned forest won't ever let us go.

Tyler touches my arm and says, "Come on, Jane. Let's look around."

I nod, pushing the thought out of my head. We search your house, eyes sweeping past the same photos that have hung on the walls for years, and, by the sink, the same blue-striped glasses I've sipped from a thousand times. It hurts to see this house ruined. The sight makes my jaw tighten and my stomach hurt. The wainscoting is warped and split, and stains darken the drywall. Last night, I didn't notice that the glass face of your me-maw's curio cabinet has been smashed in anger or confusion. Each of the ceramic figures from inside lies smashed to pieces against the far wall.

In your bedroom, the clay bodies—hollow as cicada skins, worthless as memories—hide their faces from the corruption they brought here. The beautiful sea-foam green paint peels from your walls. I remember helping you pick that color out. It looked so good in the morning sunlight. But everything here is rotten now. Everything is crumbling.

Except the guitar.

One of the bodies still clutches the Dreadnought's neck. Breaking the fingers—they crumble away in mine—I take the guitar. The strings have rusted and snapped, and mud streaks its base, but the neck and body seem intact.

"Tyler, look. Holly carried this up from the bottom of the lake, but it's not warped or rotten or anything."

"Huh. Maybe the lacquer protected it."

"Lacquer? Look around. Everything Holly touches rots.

Lacquer couldn't save it. It's got mojo, Tyler. Enough mojo to survive the drowned forest."

He crouches down and traces a finger across the abalone stars inlaid down the fretboard. "Okay, so how does it help us? How does it help Holly?"

I shake my head. "Don't know."

"Well, let's take it and get out of here." He stands up.

The sun is starting to set. Carrying the guitar, we head back to the truck and drive to Stratofortress's house.

Ultimate has returned from Britney's, and the band is sitting together in the living room. They look wrung out and hung out, eyes red from crying, pot, or both. Max asks, "Whatcha got, Jane?"

I hand the guitar over. "Check it out. It's an antique, I think."

"Yeah, this is one of the classic Dreadnoughts. See the inlays along here, little stars? And, see, it has the old-style logo." He traces the faded gold script behind the headstock, *C. F. Martin & Co. Dreadnought.* "This the guitar from the house?"

"Yeah."

"What?" LeighAnn snaps around. "You went back? Why?"

"I think this guitar is important. I'm just not sure how. But do you think you could make it play again?"

Max turns it over, gently testing the joints. "As long as the soundboard isn't broken or warped, it should play fine. Otherwise, it's a fancy piece of junk."

He swabs dry mud out of the machine heads and restrings it. Then everybody holds their breath as he balances the guitar on his thigh. Hands scabbed from meeting you last night, he dips Band-Aided fingers into the gray blur of strings, plucking out the intro to "Folsom Prison Blues."

A bird flutters in my chest. The guitar is scratched and dirty, but its voice is strong. The soundboard is full of rich harmonics. Stratofortress sings together. Shaking off the horror of last night, they come alive again, full of blood and noise.

I stand apart, but touch Tyler's elbow. "You never told them Mr. Alton won that guitar from Johnny Cash, did you?"

"Naw." Tyler laughs. "You know what a champion liar he was. You don't really believe that, do you?"

"I didn't. But then, how come the first song Max plays is a Johnny Cash song?"

"Well … wow. But how?"

"Part of its mojo." I shrug.

After Stratofortress finishes their sing-along, Tyler takes the guitar and plays a few tunes. I sit and listen, trying to figure out what the guitar means, and if we can use it to save you.

Thuck.

Something hits the window. Hobbit and Cookie howl their heads off. I look out but can't see past my own reflection in the darkening glass. Tyler stops playing and asks, "What was that?"

Thuck. The swallow leaves a star-shaped crack in the glass.

Cupping my hands to the window, I see the broken little bird splayed in the dirt. Another swoops up through the air, swallowed by the night. And there you are, a shadow among the scraps of light filling the alley. On our side of the fence, the dogs bark and snarl.

"Guys, she's here!" I yell. "Holly's here! Guys!"

"How?" Tyler asks.

"The swallows. She sent the swallows to find us. They're all over the backyard."

"Oh God, what about Hobbit and Cookie?" LeighAnn rushes past me, heading for the back door.

"Wait! LeighAnn, wait." Max bolts after her, grabbing the handle of the sliding glass door and not letting her out.

"Let go!" She punches him. Hard. Max doesn't move, just keeps yelling, "Wait a second!"

Animal yelps pierce their argument. Shoving Max aside, LeighAnn jerks open the door. The fence is rusted through, and the stamped-down dirt sprouts little flowers wherever you step, Holly. Cookie tries to bite you, and we watch you slap him. He paws at the tendrils spilling from his muzzle and won't stop crying.

LeighAnn screams. Hobbit crawls away with his tail folded against his belly. But you don't care about them, do you?

"Tyler? I heard you playing. I've been looking all over for you."

Tyler hisses to me, "I have some more chalk and lime in my truck. Keep her busy."

"How?" But he's already gone.

"I think something happened to Pa-paw. I think..."

You turn. I follow your gaze to see LeighAnn creeping along the side of the house toward Hobbit.

"Holly!" I jump off the patio, rushing to the center of the backyard. "It's me. I'm here."

You look back toward me. One eye is a smooth blue-gray

stone. The other's an empty hole. "Jane? Why do you keep hiding from me?"

"I know. I'm sorry." In my peripheral vision, I see LeighAnn grab Hobbit and run to Max. "But…but…"

Tyler rushes up and starts pouring the powder. The wind catches it, carrying it off in a long white veil before it hits the dirt.

Your voice is a muddy sob. "I need help, Jane. Stop playing stupid games!"

We stumble back from your open arms. Ultimate jerks me back. He has his cymbal stand in his other hand, its three steel legs slashing forward.

"Jane. Please. I'm sor—"

Ultimate knocks you down, pins you on your back. One of the stand's legs cuts deep into your throat, and your words are rough and breathy, "Jane, d…don't go."

"Go! I got this." Ultimate grabs the chalk and lime from Tyler. "Get Jane out of here."

Tyler takes my wrist. I cry, "Holly, I'm sor—"

"Get her out of here!"

Tyler is pulling now. Despite everything, it still hurts to turn my back on you. I manage, and we run back into the house. Max and LeighAnn are ahead of us; LeighAnn carries Hobbit.

Tyler says, "We have to bail. Get in the van. Max, the keys! The keys!"

"I know!" Max yells back.

Tyler pulls me toward the front door, but I resist. "No. The Dreadnought."

"Screw the Dreadnought! We have to—"

I tear loose and rush back, grabbing the old black guitar from the floor. It's the one clue we have.

"Jane! We have to go!"

Out the front door and into the van. LeighAnn is half out of it. She won't let go of Hobbit. Pressing her face against his fur, she moans, "Cookie. Oh, God, Cookie." Ultimate comes jogging around the side of the house with most of the cymbal stand, two of its three legs rusted away. As Max starts the engine and snaps on the headlights, there's a rush of wings—dozens of swallows scattering from the light. They land in high tree branches and the eaves of the roof, shrieking at us as Ultimate jumps into the van and we pull away.

Twenty-one

How powerful have you become, Holly? Your swallows found us, a mile from the river, and told you where we were. Are they searching the whole city for us now? We're driving away from Stratofortress's house, but it's not done. You'll come back. You'll keep coming back and coming back. You'll never let go of me.

And you've made Stratofortress into runaways too, leaving behind everything except each other. We head to Britney's apartment on Greene Street, behind Domino's.

Britney opens the door. "Hey, Steve. Um...what's up?" She glances past his shoulder at us.

"Hey, how you doing, honey?" We crowd into the living room and Steve tells her the story. Britney offers to order a pizza, but nobody's worried about food. LeighAnn holds Hobbit in her lap, and Max holds her.

"Got anything to drink?" LeighAnn asks.

Britney finds a bottle of liquor. Ultimate pours some

into a Panama City shot glass for LeighAnn and takes a swig from the bottle himself. They both twitch their heads like horses as the stuff goes down.

While Britney goes to find extra blankets for us, LeighAnn murmurs, "So what happens now?"

"We stay here tonight. And tomorrow..." Max glances at me, then away. "Tomorrow, we'll figure out what to do tomorrow."

Taking the bottle, LeighAnn pours another shot and downs it. "Jane, you can't come back. I'm sorry. Tyler, same thing."

"Come on, Lee-lee. We're not kicking them to the curb."

"Don't you remember when that thing touched you?" LeighAnn snaps. "I do. I remember pulling flowers out of—" She hits him, then starts to cry, managing, "Now it's coming to my house? Killed my damn dog."

Ultimate tries to say something; I cut him off. "She's right. Tyler, if those birds, and whatever else Holly has searching for us, found us at their house, they can find you at yours. We've got to get away. Get away from the lake, maybe from this whole stretch of river."

"You have anywhere you can go? Some family you can stay with?" Ultimate asks.

"Family that wouldn't immediately call our parents?"

"Well, we'll loan you some cash," LeighAnn says. "Plus maybe you can sell the Dreadnought. An antique like that should be worth a couple thousand."

"No." I jerk my head up. "That's—"

"Quiet," Ultimate says.

"No, we can't sell the—"

"Shut up!" Ultimate hisses. "Bird. It's one of the birds."

Perched on the window sill—a shadow against the glass— it cocks its head and stares in at us. Nobody speaks. Nobody moves.

The swallow's attention drops down to something on the sill. It pecks at it, seeming to forget about us, then flicks its forked tail and swoops back into the dull orange glow of the city.

"Did it see us? Is it going to tell Holly?"

"Well, in the first place, was it one of Holly's birds?"

"It must be."

"So what now? They followed us? Or are they looking in every window in the city?"

"And still, did it see us? It didn't look like it noticed us."

"I don't know, but tomorrow morning, you guys have to leave." Max looks at me and Tyler, squeezing LeighAnn's hand. "Sorry."

Tyler nods. This is the best thing. The only thing, really.

"Guys, I'm so sorry," Britney walks back in, arms loaded down. "I don't have enough extra blankets, just some sleeping bags."

"Don't worry. I'm used to it." I take one of the bags from her, giving her a hug in exchange.

Things settle down, and the next time I look up, Britney and Ultimate have slipped off to the bedroom. Tyler and Max decide somebody should keep watch. Tyler offers to stay up first, and he'll wake Max up at four. I stay up with him. We sit in the kitchen, the guitar on the table. It's the only clue we have—it's my last link to you. Selling it just doesn't feel right, Holly.

The apartment grows quiet, just LeighAnn's gentle snores. We keep the curtains drawn and only the light above the sink burning.

"Listen," Tyler whispers. "We're going to keep looking for answers to all this, okay? We'll sell the Dreadnought and keep looking for Dr. Frazier's missing transcripts, okay?"

I drop my face into the snug darkness between my arms. "I want to go home."

"I know."

He really doesn't, does he, Holly? Tyler doesn't have a clue what it'll be like to leave everyone behind, not even saying goodbye. He can't imagine how bad he'll want to touch their hands again, to hear their voices. He doesn't know yet, but he will soon.

He rubs my back, whispering, "It'll be okay. We're going—"

"Quit." I shove his meaty arm away.

We sit hunched into ourselves, together but alone. After a long time, I pick up the guitar, running my fingers along the strings. They sound like far away groans.

"What are you doing?" Tyler hisses. "We have to be quiet."

"I'll play quiet. Just for you and me." No pick, barely brushing the strings with the edge of my thumb. Soft snatches of songs and things I make up. The Dreadnought is big and clumsy. It was made for giants—Johnny Cash, your pa-paw— and I can hardly get my arms around it. Tyler listens until his eyes slip closed. Head in his hand, he starts snoring. It's hours until we're supposed to wake Max up. I let them all sleep for now.

I play "Down by the Riverside" so softly I have to strain to hear it. It's a song for everybody who's been cast out and cut away, everybody lost in the wilderness. Tonight, I play for me and Tyler. And LeighAnn with the job she hates, and the rest of Stratofortress. I really hope they make it someday. I play for you too, Holly. Despite all this, I still love you. I wish you knew that. I'm still chatting with you like you're right beside me because I always talked to you when I was afraid. Because how can I get through this without my best friend?

Grimacing as I shape my wounded hand into the right chords, I push through them a little smoother every time. I feel the Dreadnought's mojo as it sings about the heaviness in my bones that I don't have the words to explain. It comes from everyone who's played this guitar, every song it's sung. It makes the guitar more than what I can see with my eyes or hold in my hands.

Then God speaks. His whisper falls like an atom bomb. *Dread not.*

I hold the guitar and feel you holding it too. I can feel the magic you put into it with every song, with the first song you ever played. It was before we ever met, Holly, but the guitar holds the moment within its whorled grain.

Seven years old and an orphan and scared—scared in a way you didn't even have words for. One day, your pa-paw folds his calloused fingers over your soft ones. Together, you strum loud and laugh and the music makes you feel brave.

You squint through the sound hole, searching for that magic. The guitar is just wood and metal strings, nothing mysterious. You keep searching, though. You touch the curling gold letters behind the headstock, sounding them out.

C. F. Martin & Co. Dreadnought.

Dread not.

God laid His hand upon your head and made a promise. Dread not, and even when you couldn't be strong, music would make you as stubborn as spring. Dread not, Holly, and music would be your deep roots. You would survive drought and freeze. You played and played that old Dreadnaught until your fingers blistered and bled and calloused. You kept your end of the covenant. When your me-maw died, you almost forgot, but I helped you remember. I helped you decorate—dedicate—your new guitar.

Fear not.

In Britney's kitchen, I start playing fearlessly, strings biting my fingertips. We just have to make you remember again.

Tyler's head jerks up. "Jane! Jane, quit!"

"I know why Auntie Peake's prayer didn't work!" I say. "Holly had her own way of praying. She connected to God through music. See? Dreadnought. Like 'fear not.' Like she painted on her guitar. We just have to get her to pray her way."

He blinks at me, eyes dull with sleep. "Huh?"

I explain everything, slower this time. In the living room, LeighAnn and Max sit up and listen.

"You want to get her to play music?" LeighAnn asks. "How do you even try without getting killed? And even if she remembers, how can that help?"

"If Holly remembers anything, it's music. Music made her feel close to God." I laugh as it all slides so easily into place. "That's why Auntie Peake's prayer wouldn't work; Holly talked to God, heard God, in music. So if we get her to play, reconnect her to God, she'll find her way out of the drowned forest."

"You haven't answered the 'without getting killed' part."

"We have to try," Tyler says. "Me and Jane, we loved her. We owe her. But you guys don't owe Holly anything. You guys should stay clear."

"Are you kidding me?" The bedroom door swings open. Ultimate steps out, zipping up his pants. "Back when we were in the Banana Hammocks, Holly came to our first-ever gig. Can't leave a fan hanging."

"Thanks, man." Tyler gives him a shoulder-bumping half-hug.

Max and LeighAnn look at each other. Max says, "If Steve dies, we gotta find a new drummer."

"Yeah ... wanna ask Davis?"

"He's in Gypsy Fingers now. What about Twitchy?"

"Twitchy's a pothead. He'll never come to practice. Maybe Karen?"

"I'm not putting up with that Britpop crap."

LeighAnn groans and kicks out of the sleeping bag. "Forget it. Easier just to keep this one alive."

Ultimate Steve bumps shoulders with her too. "Leave Hobbit here. I'll write a note for Britney."

Slipping on shoes, grabbing the Dreadnought, we head out into the night.

Twenty-two

When you prayed like us, did you feel anything at all, Holly? Or was it just endless dark behind your eyelids and clasped hands itching for steel strings?

The lights still burn in Stratofortress's house. I walk through carrying your pa-paw's guitar. Ultimate grabs a mic stand and follows me.

"Holly?" Through the kitchen, out to the patio. "Holly?"

But your latest body lies still, the cymbal stand's rusted leg planted deep in its chest. Ultimate didn't just draw a magic circle around you, he poured the chalk and lime on top of you like he was salting a slug.

Tyler kicks at a clump of pokeweed that's sprung up where Cookie died. There's nothing left of the dog except a few brittle bones. Then we go back to the others, standing on the patio.

"So what now?" LeighAnn asks. "Just sit around and wait until she comes back?"

Tyler shakes his head. "Every time she dies, her soul

gets pulled back to the drowned forest. That's where she must be now. We need to go to her, now that we're ready."

"But what if she's scared and angry?" I ask. "What if she doesn't want to come out of the water?"

"We'll make sure she can't ignore us," Max says. "Load up the gear. We'll bring the two-by-twelve and the mini colossal."

"Where are you going to plug in an amp by the river?"

"I'm an electrician, Lee-Lee. We *always* know where to plug it in." When LeighAnn rolls her eyes, Max grins. "That was a joke. A dirty one. See, by 'plug it in' I could have been referring—"

"I got it, cowboy. I just didn't want it."

LeighAnn and Ultimate have loaded and unloaded the gear so many times, they work without a word passed between them. They only have to speak to tell me or Tyler where stuff fits and how to strap down the amps.

While the rest of us load the van, Max buries Cookie's bones in the backyard. We're sitting in the van when he comes around, wiping his hands on his jeans. "Ready?"

LeighAnn nods, sniffling back tears for Cookie.

The streets are empty. The van's pale reflection slithers across darkened windows of law offices and the Starbucks. I'll always remember our nights downtown, Holly. Just running around, burning to be loud and be alive. Sometimes I'd look up and there wasn't any sky. The moon was hidden. City lights blinded us to the stars. I'd look up into dead black forever. You saw it too, didn't you? It's why you always laughed louder than me, howled and sang. You were the most alive person I ever knew. I get it now. It was the only way you had to keep all that horrible nothing from reaching inside you.

I have to remember that tonight. Tonight and the rest of my life.

They padlock the gate to Veterans Park after sundown. Pulling up, Max says, "There's a hacksaw in the toolbox by your foot there."

"Got it." Hopping out, LeighAnn cuts through the lock and waves us through.

We drive behind the baseball diamonds, the van swaying hard as Max pulls off the paved road and onto the grass near the shore.

Hidden in the tall grass, crickets thrum like a pulse. As I help set the amps on the ground, the van's headlights are warm against my skin. They stretch our shadows out across the land and the water.

Kneeling by one of the stadium light poles, Max opens the steel panel in its base with a special wrench. He hooks up the amps with alligator clamps, and they fill with their electric, wasp-nest murmur. Tyler pours the last of the chalk and lime on the grass, sketching out a stage around the band. Then he stands back and watches them finish setting up.

"Tyler," I say. "You need to play with them."

"Huh? No way. We may only have one chance at this."

"But you need to play or else Holly won't know it's us. Remember?"

He remembers, his face growing pale as wax paper in the lamplight. He starts twisting the plastic bag in his hands nervously. "Jane, what if I mess up like last time?"

"You won't."

"What if I do? Holly might not come. Or she might end up hurting somebody else."

I look at him, choosing my words very carefully. "I never liked you much," I say.

Tyler snorts. "Gee, thanks."

"Well, I didn't. I thought you were a loud-mouth and a goof-off. And I figured Holly just hung out with you because you were a good musician, like, you could talk about music and guitars and stuff that I didn't really know anything about." It's hard to admit. I usually think I have most people figured out, and lately, it seems like I'm wrong a lot of the time. "But she loved you because of your heart, because she knew you'd never let her down."

He turns away, squeezing her eyes shut. "Except I did. I let her die, Jane."

"No. That was an accident. You're not responsible for that, only what you've done since. And since then you've stuck by her, stuck by me. I couldn't have done any of this without you."

He wipes his eyes with his palm. "I still don't know how that's going to keep me from messing up now."

"She loved you because of your heart. *That's* what called her to you in the first place. Go and play with the band. Make a mistake or two, but as long as that heart comes through in the music, Holly will come. I know it."

He nods and hugs me. No half-hug either. Tyler squeezes me tight, almost lifting me off my feet.

Ultimate yells, "Come on, guys. We're ready."

Turning, Tyler steps into the circle. LeighAnn hands

him his guitar, and Stratofortress is ready for a very strange gig. Except beyond the lights, there's just the choppy water. The audience hasn't shown up yet.

I look over my shoulder at Tyler. "How about 'Down by the Riverside'? That seems right."

Tyler nods and starts to play, skipping staccato notes across the water like stones. Stratofortress comes in, backing Tyler up with a wall of rhythm and bass. I stand there holding the Dreadnought.

The Dread Not.

I sing along with the band. "*I'm gonna lay down my heavy load, down by the riverside, down by the riverside, down by the riverside…*"

Fish start breaking the surface of the water, flashing silver. One lands on the bank, flops and gasps, stranded among the Queen Anne's lace blooming between the stones. Shadows of birds jerk through the headlight beams.

The waves grow rough, a hundred foamy lips smacking against the rocks. The stink grows too. It's death, but it's not cold and not silent. It's fertile black death as warm as flesh, hungry to feed new green shoots. It's the last truth, isn't it, Holly? As absolute as life ending in death, every death brings new life.

"*I'm gonna put on my long white robe, down by the riverside, down by the riverside, down by the riverside. I'm gonna put on my…* Holly … hey …"

"Jane?"

The music scatters to silence behind us. "It's me, Holly. And Tyler. He's here too."

"Why do you keep leaving? I need help."

"I'm sorry. I'm here now. I won't leave this time." But before you cross the circle, I yell, "Wait! Holly, look. I brought your pa-paw's Dreadnought. Remember? Dread Not? Don't you remember?"

"It's broken. I tried to play... it's broken, broken."

"No, my friend just had to re-string it. Listen." I play "Mary Had a Little Lamb" through steady, certain fingers.

The gash of your mouth bends into something like a smile. "When'd you learn that?"

"This week. I've learned a lot of... a lot."

Twisting your fingers around each other, you stare around. "I got lost. We were at the bluff, but I got lost in the forest. I need to go home."

"It'll be okay. Here, you remember how to play, don't you?" Stepping across the white line, I meet you on the border between water and land, between life and death. I push Johnny Cash's guitar into your hands.

Fingers travel across the frets. They trace the faded logo on the headstock, just like I know they did that first time you played, years ago. You strum a loose, buzzing chord, and hope swells in my chest. Another chord. Then, "I need to go home. Let's go home, Jane."

"You have to remember how to play, Holly. Just remember."

"No!"

The swallows cry out as you throw the guitar away. The clay bank crumbles underneath us, and we both tumble to the water. My knee smashes against algae-slick rocks. A wave crashes down on my back, then washes back out. Sputtering, I feel the river thirsty to slurp us down.

I scuttle back toward land, dragging my leg. My knee bleeds freely, hot blood spilling across goose-pimpled flesh. You grab my arm with fingers worn down to driftwood spurs, keeping me from reaching the dry bank. We kneel together in the shallow water, on the tip of the river's tongue. The waves have washed your face smooth.

"I have to get home, please," you say. "Pa-paw's going to be worried."

"You can't." The black water swirls around our ankles. Pale flowers push up from my scratches, but I ignore the feeling of their roots probing beneath my skin. "Holly, you can't go home anymore. I'm sorry, but you got lost in the drowned forest, and nobody can get back from there."

"Stop! I have to go home!" Another waist-high wave smashes into us as you scream.

"You can't, Holly. But you can go *through*. You have to go through the drowned forest to the other side."

"But you have to go alone." Tyler is beside us, and he has the Dreadnought. "You have to let go of Jane, sweetheart. Please, please."

"No ... not alone. Please, I can't go alone."

"Sure you can." Tyler offers her the guitar. "Dread not, remember? Fear not."

"Tyler ... "

"Your pa-paw's waiting for you. Your mom and dad, your me-maw, they're all waiting for you on the other side. Just let go of Jane, okay? Please?"

You take the guitar. Tyler takes my arm. The rest of Stratofortress all grab ahold and haul me onto the grass. We watch and listen as you pluck out "Down by the Riverside" on the lonely guitar.

Then the swallows begin singing in harmony. Crickets chirp out a distortion-thick rhythm, following your lead in perfect cut time. The rough waves strike the rocks in a slap-crash bass line. The song fills the darkness. The strings rust and snap under your fingers. You strum like they're still there, playing all of deafening creation.

I'm gonna lay down my heavy load, down by the riverside, down by the riverside, down by the riverside.
I'm gonna lay down my heavy load, down by the riverside.
I'm gonna study war no more.

Then you look up, at something just over our heads, speaking to somebody we can't see. Your smile on that rough face—I'd almost forgotten how beautiful it was. When you slump sideways, folding down to the rocks, I gasp and try to stand. Tyler holds me. "It's okay, Jane. Let her go."

The birds and crickets keep singing. The waves crash down, snatching you—no, just the lump of clay you left behind—back down to the drowned forest.

"The guitar!" Ultimate splashes after the Dreadnought as it tumbles, black against black, toward the center of the lake.

Nature's song goes on a little longer, and then the swallows start flying off—one, three, then the great rustling storm of them all at once. The cricket-rhythm tumbles back to the ordinary drone of insects again.

When I fell, a rock tore open the skin below my knee. As I try to stand, icy bolts shoot up into my stomach and make me want to puke. Flopping back to the ground, I start plucking the flowers from the scratches in my arm, sucking my breath as I pull out the roots. Now that you're finally gone, the pain and panic I kept squashed down in my chest overtakes me all at once. I have to keep wiping tears away to see the flowers. My hands shake so bad, I can't pull them out anyway.

"It's okay, don't cry." Crouching beside me, Tyler helps pluck the flowers. "We'll get them all out. Don't cry."

"I'm not crying for that. It's because—ow!" I grit my teeth as he yanks the last flower. "It's because Holly's gone to Heaven. She's not lost anymore."

He grins and nods. "We did it."

And suddenly I'm laughing. As the pain and panic rush out, the only thing left in my chest is a trilling joy. While Tyler and a sopping wet Ultimate—Dreadnought in one hand—help me to the van, I'm crying and laughing and wincing with every step. I'm a bloody, muddy mess, and I can't stop singing.

"*I'm gonna put on my long white robe, down by the riverside, down by the riverside, down by the riverside…*" I sit on the floor of the van, emptying water out of the Dreadnought's sound hole. While Stratofortress tosses equipment and cables in all around me, they sing along.

"*… I'm gonna put on my long white robe, down by the riverside. I'm gonna study war no more…*"

Twenty-three

I'm going home. I want to be clean and wearing my own clothes, without bags under my eyes. I'll settle for being clean.

I gobble some Tylenol and step into the shower. My knee hurts too much to stand, though, so I ease down to the tub floor and inspect the curved cut under the pelting water, then clean away the worst of the dirt and dried blood.

You're already with your family—your mom and dad and grandparents met you on that distant shore. That makes me happy while I work clumps of mud out of my hair.

It's Sunday morning and almost time for church, but LeighAnn wants to cook me and Tyler breakfast before we leave. It's the first time she's offered to cook anything, so I let her. While the sausage sizzles in the pan, I hand the Dreadnought to Tyler. "Here. You should have this."

He takes it reverently. "Thanks. I—I'll take good care of it. Get Dad to built a display cabinet or some—"

"What? No." I snatch the guitar back. "It doesn't belong in a case. It belongs onstage, Tyler."

"But it belonged to Johnny Cash." Then, in a softer voice, "Holly used to play it."

"Exactly. It's too valuable not to be played. That mojo needs to be heard. So either you promise to play it—often, and where people can hear—or I'll keep it and start my own band."

"You know, like, one and a half songs."

"And I will play the heck out of those one and a half songs."

Tyler sighs, then glances around sheepishly at Stratofortress. "So, do you think maybe you could give me one more shot at joining the band?"

Stratofortress looks at one another. LeighAnn says, "Well, we're doing Dave's house show again this year, aren't we?"

Max nods.

Ultimate Steve speaks up. "Come on, guys. If he can keep his cool playing for a ghost, he deserves another shot."

Max nods some more. "Sure, big guy. We can give you another shot."

Tyler's too exhausted to get excited, but he grins and bumps Max's fist. "Thanks, guys."

We eat our breakfast, and then it's time for me and Tyler to go. I hug everybody goodbye, all of them all at once. LeighAnn tells me to come back any time I want to jam.

I sniffle. "Thanks. Thank you for everything." I limp out to Tyler's truck and won't let him help me into the passenger seat.

Driving to the church, he asks, "So, think your folks will be mad? You going to be in trouble?"

"If I am, I'll manage. I've managed worse."

We pass by the dam. There are already fishing boats out there, lines sinking down into the drowned forest. The church parking lot is full, but Tyler finds a spot. The buildings look exactly the same except thinner somehow, smaller. But church isn't a building, is it, Holly? All our time lost in the wilderness, God never left us. He sent helpers, but I called them herpes sponges. The way home was in front of me the whole time—plain as the interstate—but I had to become somebody new before I could see it.

Unbuckling my seat belt, I say, "Maybe you shouldn't come in with me. If they figure out you knew where I was the whole time—"

"I don't care. I want to go in with you."

Sometimes, with some people, there's no reason to act brave. "Thanks."

I make it up the steps and open the door. Deacon Colefield is holding a stack of church bulletins. "Good morn..." His fixed grin slides down. "Jane?"

"Hello, Mr. Colefield. Good morning." I limp past him before he asks where I've been.

The congregation sings "All The Way My Savior Leads Me." I limp up the side aisle, and only a few people bother to glance around. Pastor Wesley sees me. I don't hate him, Holly, even though I thought I did. It's not his fault he doesn't know how deep the river's mojo really runs or how big God really is. I give him my best Ultimate Steve sneering smile, and for just a moment he falters, the song rolling along without him.

Then Yuri turns. Those chocolate-brown eyes that see everything watch me calmly, like he's been expecting me.

"Hey, pal," I whisper. Then Tim shouts my name, diving toward me. The whole family spills out of the pew, talking over one another. Mom starts crying. They all touch me, grab ahold of me, afraid I might disappear again.

Epilogue

The woman bursts from the water, a halo of droplets winking in the sun. She wobbles backward, and the deacon steadies her. Her skin is shiny, pearly pink. Her expression is one of the most beautiful things I've ever seen.

The deacon helps her to the shore and into her husband's arms. They hug while Pastor Wesley beckons the next white-robed woman into the river. His shirt darkens with water. Her mouth opens wide in a sob or laugh. Rivercall becomes just the two of them, too intimate to watch.

I focus on the steel strings thundering under my fingers, the swell and smash of the familiar song.

"... *down by the riverside, down by the riverside. I'm gonna put on my long white robe, down by the riverside...*"

I borrowed Tyler's Vox amp, just for today. It sounds so delicious, Holly. I add a fast lick heading into the bridge. Risking a little pride, I glance up to see if Max noticed. He and LeighAnn sing and clap along in time. Max gives me a quick thumbs-up.

One by one, the converts slip underwater, vanish into the silence and chill of death for just a moment. Then they emerge, one by one, brilliant and new.

By the end, I'm slippery with sweat. Pastor Wesley leads a quick prayer and thanks the Ladies' Auxiliary for helping out. When he says my name, everybody cheers. I don't know how to deal with that, so I grin and wave, then act busy winding up cords.

The congregation heads toward the picnic tables, piling plates with chicken and potato salad and steaming ears of sweet corn. Max and LeighAnn come to help me load gear back into the church van.

"Pretty good, Jane."

"Thanks."

"C'mon. Let's see." LeighAnn holds her hand up, and I press mine against hers. A year's worth of playing has left half-moon calluses on each fingertip, as shiny as the Cheshire Cat's grin, as beautiful as battle scars.

Has it really been a year since I ran away, Holly? My family still doesn't know what happened, just that I emerged a week later, filthy, cut up, and wanting a guitar. I wish I could tell them. I wish they'd believe me. For now, though, it will remain a wedge of silence between us.

At least they didn't punish me or anything. They made me see Dr. Haq once a week, and he made me sign that "no harm contract" promising I wouldn't run away again. After three months, he scribbled on a prescription sheet and handed it to Mom. *Buy her a guitar. Give her time to play every day.*

We went downtown, and I picked out my guitar—the same silver-haunted green as the river. After that, I was officially cured.

Well, I still talk to you every day, so I'm probably still a tiny bit nuts. I just don't think there's much helping it.

And I rarely feel God's presence like I did before, when we were kids. I still pray every day, but I can count on one hand the times I've felt consumed with His love. I don't think there's any helping that either. It's part of growing up, Holly. We get older, and God makes us search Him out more and more. It's up to us to find His image in a band of struggling rockers, His voice in an autumn-crisp A-minor chord.

Lifting the Vox into the van with LeighAnn, I grunt, "How's Ultimate? I meant to call him yesterday."

"Acting like a big baby. His foot's mostly healed, but he lies around playing video games and begging me to make him sandwiches."

"You know, after cutting off a finger, you think he'd be more careful."

"Guy suffers for his art." Panting, LeighAnn slumps against the middle seat. "Roadie work is a heck of a lot harder in pumps."

"Yeah."

"Also, when you can't cuss."

I snicker. LeighAnn just popped up one Sunday at church, Holly. I felt a tap on my shoulder, and there she was, grinning behind her huge Jackie O hangover glasses. She sat with Tyler and slipped out as soon as service ended. The week after that, her and Max both came.

Now they come most Sundays, usually straight from wherever they spent Saturday night, singing praise, stinking of beer and stale cigarette smoke. Neither of them has decided to get baptized yet, and Max says he just likes the music. But I keep praying maybe their wandering is coming to an end.

Done loading, we get lunch. Holly, can you smell Mrs. Chandler's chicken? It's so good, it makes you jealous of the chicken. Here we all are, wandering around, trying to figure out what God wants for us. But the chicken's purpose in life is so clear—to be soaked in buttermilk and fried up by Mrs. Chandler.

Tyler is talking with Hannah Marie. He tells her his plans now that he's graduated, and she inspects the silhouette of an airplane tattooed on his inner forearm. When she spots me, she starts hopping in place. "Jane! Oh wow, you were so good!"

"Thanks."

"I could never stand up there and do something like that. And you did it and didn't even look nervous."

"Well..."

"All right, I'm going to go eat. But hey." She jabs Tyler in the arm. "You can't just disappear now you've graduated, okay? You better email me sometime."

"I will. I promise."

"Good. Looking forward to it."

I get some green beans and don't say anything until Hannah Marie has bounced off. Then, "You know she likes you, right?"

Tyler scoops the meringue off his lemon meringue pie. "She's always like that."

"She's always like that around *you*."

He scrunches his forehead at me, glances back at Hannah Marie.

"Go invite her to Friday's gig."

He stalls a little while longer, then goes to talk to her. After he's gone, LeighAnn says, "They do look really cute together."

"Sure. Plus, you see how chatty she is. If she likes Stratofortress, she'll tell everybody. That word-of-mouth is what you guys need to start drawing big crowds."

"It really scares me how under all the Sesame Street stuff, you have the heart of a record exec."

We sit on the rocks by the shore, balancing our plates in our laps. We eat our chicken and joke around. Kicking my sandals off, I stir my toes through the cool water. I wish for the millionth time that you could have known these guys, Holly. And I wish you could have known me, too, the person I've become and all the songs I'm learning to play.

I miss you, Holly, and I'll love you forever. But death can't stop life. Even when something sinks down to the drowned forest, something new will always emerge from the shimmering, restless river.

About the Author

Kristopher Reisz grew up in Alabama surrounded by old music and deep wildernesses ripe for exploring. While learning to write he worked as a paramedic, a third-shift short-order cook, and in a mental hospital. He's written two previous books, a bunch of short stories, and currently lives beside a slow-moving river.